Holiday Sampler

Holiday Sampler

A Holiday Anthology from the Writers Cooperative of the Pacific Northwest

Published by
Writers Cooperative of the
Pacific Northwest

writers-coop.com

Holiday Sampler from the Writers Cooperative of the Pacific Northwest

First Printing, 2018

ISBN: 9781723907340

Permissions:
An-cake-estry, Welcoming With Gratitude, Deep Into Winter, ©2018 Toni Kief; The End of the Alphabet, Christmas Lights, Peace On Earth, Boxing Day, We Need a Little Christmas, ©2018 Susan Brown; Holiday Pearl ©2018 R.Todd Fredrickson; The Gift ©2018 Stephanie Larkin (Published by Ahadi Publications); A New Winter Song, Old Old Coat ©2018 Roland Trenary; The Christmas Mug, ©2016 Linda Jordan (Published by Metamorphosis Press), The Best Little Christmas Ever © 2013 by Linda Jordan (Published by Metamorphosis Press), Marta and the Christmas Cat © 2016 Linda Jordan (Published by Metamorphosis Press), We Wish You a Merry Christmas © 2014 by Linda Jordan (Published by Metamorphosis Press); Twenty Cookies and a Plane Ticket, Winter's Day, Fall, ©2018 Celena Davis-Dunivent; Gift of the Stars, A Pacific Northwest Winter, ©2018 Sonya Rhen.

Editor: Sonya Rhen
Illustrations: ©2018 Roland Trenary
Paperback Book Formatting: Roland Trenary
Cover Design: Heather McIntyre heather.mcintyre@coverandlayout.com

Published by the Writers Cooperative of the Pacific Northwest

For more works by these and other members of the Writers Cooperative of the Pacific Northwest visit their website.

http://writers-coop.com/

This book is dedicated to aspiring writers
and to you,
our fabulous readers.

Writers Cooperative of the Pacific Northwest is an author-owned, author-operated cooperative made up of writers, storytellers and creative minds dedicated to the craft of writing, publishing, and marketing intellectual property. As writers, we have asked the question: how can authors take advantage of and profit from the changes taking place in publishing today? By recognizing the unique opportunity we have to help shape that future through an author-owned and operated cooperative that empowers its author-owners in any activity related to the process of creating, publishing, marketing and advertising their work (while retaining the greatest percentage of their profits). If you would like to become a part of WCPNW, or simply continue the conversation, we welcome the opportunity to share our ideas.

TABLE OF CONTENTS

Toni Kief
Marysville, WA

Toni started writing near retirement. She's published three novels, is writing a fourth, and is gathering research for a fifth. Most of what she writes is fiction whose protagonists are often older women. She is a founder of the Writers Cooperative of the Pacific Northwest; they work as a team on better manuscripts, marketing, and publishing.
www.tonikief.com

An-cake-estry
Welcoming With Gratitude
Deep Into Winter

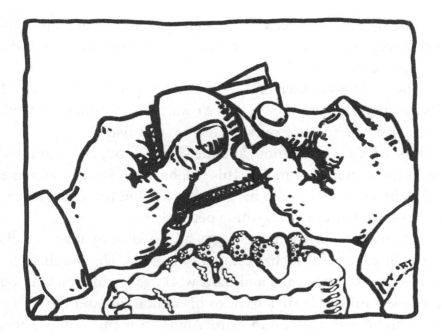

An-cake-estry

Walking through the grocery store at daylight, Richard's heart fills with memories as he refolds the yellowed slip of paper stained by time and spills. Maybe it was the end of his marriage or the beginning of winter that accounts for his nostalgia. He doesn't look for an explanation. All through the night, he was awash in the memories of his grandmother. The morning started drenched in the guilt of how he was too busy, too distracted and he allowed decades and traditions to slip away. Not sure this plan would work, there was nothing to lose.

A quick check of his watch and it is time to call his only daughter. In two rings Pilar's sweet voice answers. Richard could hear the background demands of her life begging for attention, so he hurries to the point. "Pilar, remember the stories of your great-grandmother, Abuela Maria and how she welcomed winter?"

She sighs. "I felt cheated as a young girl, you would talk about her ceremony, and I wanted to be part of it. The stories sounded amazing even then."

Richard knows then and there that the plan would work. "Is Ricky busy tomorrow?" He doesn't wait for a response. "Would you allow him to come over? I'd like to start again."

She offers no hesitation, and the tradition of generations will welcome winter once more. This will be his five-year-old name-sake's first visit alone with his grandfather, and Richard whispers a prayer that he does everything perfectly.

He reaches for the ingredients, all listed in Spanish, on the scrap of paper and Richard notices his hand. He visualizes her hands, marked by years, and hard work, gathering, picking out the best vanilla. He slips back to his childhood and the excitement to be with her and to help. Abuela was the only one who called him Ricardo, she spoke little English, but language is no barrier for the love only a grandparent can give. Even though he is still shopping, he can feel the heat of her kitchen as he prepares for tomorrow.

Saturday morning his grandson arrives right on time. The boy runs to the door followed by his mother. The energy changes as soon as Ricky walks into Richard's apartment. Pilar rushes to kiss her son's forehead. "Remember like we talked, be good and to pay attention so you can teach me next year."

The small boy looks serious and agrees to the heavy responsibility. The excitement in his face lights the room as she winks at her father, turning to leave. Richard blinks back tears, listening to her hum as she returns to the car. Opening the car door, Pilar waves and calls back. "Dinner will be at six. Don't be late."

The team of Ricardos start immediately, as Abuelo Ricardo turns on the oven, then tucks dish towels around both their waists. As one they use soap and lukewarm water to wash their hands.

All of the tools are lined up on the counter and a stool waits for the boy. Ricky needs two hands to handle great-great grandmother Maria's sifter, filling the bowl with flour. Abuelo Ricardo adds a little salt and baking powder and cherishes the determination as the boy wrestles his task. Together they set aside the flour and prepare a second bowl, the large stoneware one Richard remembered most from his youth. He was a young man when Abuela Maria died, and the only things he asked for on those dark days was her baking utensils. Little Ricardo holds the electric mixer and creams the soft butter and sugar. They both smell the vanilla before pouring it into the fluffy mass. The two Ricardos talk sharing stories of the ancestors and the country the family left nearly eighty years ago. Together, they crack five eggs into a teacup one at a time. Abuelo picks out the shells, and then the eager boy pours them in and mixes it all together. They high five each other about no significant spills then pour milk into the measuring cup, and today Richard understands his Abuela's moist eyes, they came from pride.

Patiently Richard pours the dry ingredients a little at a time into the sweet golden mixture, and little Ricardo revs the beater again. Holding the giant bowl, they share the duty of scraping the batter into a well-worn cake pan.

Once in the oven, time seems to stand still. Finally, the rich smell of the pastel fills their noses and they return to watch the cake transform through the tiny window. Slowly it raises, and when the cake bounces back at a gentle touch, Richard takes it out. Using only a towel to protect his hands like his grandmother always did, she was a superhero, and those are big shoes to fill.

Little Ricardo left his toys to touch the warmth and squeals as the cake bounces back. No one will know this cake is dusted with tiny fingerprints. The tension is palpable as Abuelo, for the first time, flips the creation onto a platter. Their laughter blends, filling the apartment as little Ricardo pokes holes in the cake with a fork. The anticipation of tasting it is hell, but they have more mixing to do; baking is busy work.

Richard is nervous as he picks up the cans of evaporated and condensed milk, then a carton of heavy cream. Hearing her voice from his heart, he repeats her words, "Uno, dos, tres leches." Her essence still lives manifesting again in the little bottle of vanilla they smell a second time before it's added to the milks.

The fragrance takes them back to the time before either birth as they pour the milks onto their handiwork. This cake, a sensual pleasure of sights and smells, adds to the agonizing lesson of patience.

Now finished, they cover the cake with the lid from the roaster pan and some aluminum foil. The team of Ricardos arrives just in time for dinner. Little Ricardo keeps the cake hidden, so it can be a surprise when it is time. Pilar has also been busy all day. She serves a traditional meal, and little Ricardo's daddy brags how Mommy made the tortillas by hand. The family laughs and share delicious food and more stories of those that were gone, but live on inside of them.

Once they are done, Richard helps clear the table and calls from the kitchen, "Ricardo I need you." Abuelo Ricardo gives the little man a knife, and under his loving gaze, the boy cuts strawberries into irregular shapes. Using a small bowl, they whip even more sweetened heavy cream and slather it over the cake. Stealing only one taste, Little Ricardo places all the other pieces of fruit on his masterpiece. Abuelo corrects nothing.

Still feeling the pride fifty years later Richard sees the ghost faces of generations light up in the dining room when they present the cake. The rich texture of the memory kisses his mouth as he takes the first bite. Next year little Ricardo will help teach his mother of the same life-affirming cake, and Richard builds the taste of unconditional love with another generation.

Welcoming With Gratitude

We watched the new people since the first day they anchored the ship off of Cape Cod. They were unaware of our presence. We are the people of the first light, the Wampanoags. We lived and took care of the Massachuset, which means by the range of hills. They called their group the Separatists, later were called Pilgrims. Upon the time they landed, men went ashore to search for a place to live. Once we recognized they brought women and children, we knew they were not there to conquer or kidnap, but to make homes.

After weeks of searching, they found an abandoned village, Patuxet. It had been devastated by a plague brought to us by the white traders and trappers. In our homeland over half of our members were lost due to the unknown illnesses. All of the neighbors in Patuxet had died over two years before. The village remained empty, which is our custom. The Separatists all moved to it and named it Plymouth after the city they had sailed from in England.

Once we were sure they were peaceful, we made contact. The Separatists weren't like the others that came before. In the first year, we watched as they buried half of the original numbers. They tried to keep the losses secret, but there is no escaping our eyes. The diminishing community worked very hard to make shelters and begin a new life. We watched when they stole some of our stores of seeds that were buried waiting for spring. We were confident this group was accepting and looking for a home, peace and a place to live their religion. Our chief, Massasoit, made a treaty with their leaders. According to the agreement if a Wampanoag broke the peace, he would be sent to Plymouth for punishment; if a colonist broke the law, he would likewise be sent to the Wampanoags.

Before the spring, we took Tisquantum to meet with them. He had been captured and taken away years before. When he returned all of his family was lost in the same village the Separatist inhabited. He could speak their language, and he chose to work with them. They called him Squanto, and he taught them how to plant fields as we do. There should be three seeds, a corn kernel, a pea to grow up the stalk, and squash to cover the ground and keep away weeds. To this, we add a fish that makes the soil fertile. He spent much time with them, and because of him, they learned of the richness of the land and sea.

The Separatist hard working and very serious. They were here nearly a year, and we witnessed the successes. The men built many shelters and a wall on the hill. As with our tribe, the women manage the gardens and fields. It was the labor of the women that made for the fortune of the plentiful harvest.

One day, we heard much shooting of guns. Fearing our new neighbors were under attack we went to give aid. We discovered they were celebrating the harvest. The leader, Mr. Brewster, extended an invitation to Massasoit and the braves to stay and eat. We learned they only honor holidays found in the Bible, and this was one of the few. Our numbers were greater than theirs as Massasoit had ninety braves with him. There wouldn't be enough food for this three-day event. Four of our hunters went out and returned with five deer that we presented as a gift.

Women of our community did not come with us, we didn't expose them or the children to possible danger. The women of the settlers only numbered four, as the others had died in the dark time after the ship landed. This small group of women and the girls did not participate in the games, but worked continually grinding grain, baking cornbread, succotash, soups, and pies. These few roasted the fish and fowl the men had gathered. They used the fireplaces for cooking and a community oven that was watched over by one of the older girls. Once the venison was skinned and butchered, every part was roasted over a fire and consumed.

We, the men and boys, played games and tests of skill. The celebration went on for three days. The women did not participate, and rose before everyone, to prepare the repast. Through the days they continued to bake, roast and cook for the multiple meals needed for the festivities. They did not sit with us, and when they were not making food, they were cleaning and preparing for the next meal. At times we wondered if they slept or ate.

After the three days, we returned to our home villages and continued to live in peace with this new gathering of workers and families for many years. The Pilgrim-Wampanoag treaty was honored for over fifty years.

This may have been one of the few Thanksgivings that the Natives of this continent celebrated. They were treated as equals and accepted as neighbors. The actual historical story has been simplified and romanticized over the years. It also served as the first recorded three-day weekend.

Deep Into Winter

Routine, rut, grind, I don't care what it is called I'm stuck. Claiming to be in the fall of my life, I privately admit the truth; I'm in deep winter. All of the extra time that comes with this current status slips away in three winks. I waste time on Facebook and with old friends as we join to look back through a catalog of incarnations. In desperate need of new memories, I sit in my rocker listening to the radio, ignorant of podcasts and where they are grown.

Today, I shake off the cobwebs of the time gone by and remember the spontaneous, action me. I was knee deep in half-planned schemes and letting details fall where they may: the memory of diving utterly unprepared into risk and sometimes thrilled by incredible results. I always challenged the mundane while building a PG-17 resume of rom-com episodes with survivable heartbreak and political marches.

I didn't see this coming. I just woke up covered in dust and suffering from adequate sleep. My much younger, closest friend, complains about her knees and low back pain. A wild night starts at four in the afternoon with the happy hour specials. It all changes in a moment, I swear the wrinkles came from sleeping crooked, and they should shake out tomorrow morning. Or was it that night a 20-something offered me a pity dance to the joy of his friends? Was I young the hour, the day, the week before, and they missed it? My feet still feel the ache of walking for miles in uncomfortable but darling shoes. I have forgotten the last time I borrowed a safety pin to wrangle a low-cut dress into social acceptance. I yearn for laughter with friends without peeing. Where are the stupid ideas and the brass tits to go for it? I loved the results of nothing working out as planned providing even better results. Apparently, that one night I went to bed before the bar closed and I slipped into ordinary on the side of the high-speed highway.

Don't take me wrong, I'm not unhappy; I'm just a little bored. My passion and nerve live on, but earlier and slower. I'm having trouble climbing over the edges of this ditch to stare a new chapter square in the eye.

I refuse to let stagnation be my epilogue, so I've developed a plan. Next time someone says, "Do you want the usual?" My answer needs to be, "No thank you. I'll have the unusual, please." Some of the greatest holidays are in the winter season.

Susan Brown
Lake Stevens, WA

Susan Brown's books ripple with strong characters and fast action – whether fantasies, teen adventures, or romances (written with Anne Stephenson as Stephanie Browning). Dragons, bullies, and falling in love (plus all the ins and outs of contemporary life) can be found in Susan Brown's novels! She is a founding member of the WCPNW.

www.Susanbrownwrites.com
www.Stephaniebrowningromance.com

The End of the Alphabet
Christmas Lights
Peace On Earth
Boxing Day
We Need a Little Christmas

The End of the Alphabet

Nobody was coming. Katie Zeferelli dropped the phone on the carpet and flung herself backwards onto the sofa. A poof of Salvation Army special wafted upward and the Charlie Brown Christmas tree dropped a few needles in response to her sobs. Her career as an actress (possibly as a human being) had been stillborn; her family had gone on a cruise for Christmas, and the last of her fabulous new friends had just cancelled on her Holly Jolly Christmas party.

"What do I have to do to make my life work?" she demanded. Her cat Zed briefly opened one eye, then twisted and licked his butt.

"That's not an option," Katie snapped. The Titanic was her current life metaphor. Lots of self-proclaimed fanfare and then *Blam*. Disaster. Well, maybe not as much a disaster as the old guy clerking at the convenience store. His badge didn't say Tom, or Jose, or Billy-Bob – it said MR ZADROOZNY. The end of the alphabet (she related), the tag-end of life, the bottom of the business barrel and he insisted on being a Mister. Katie liked that. She liked it a lot.

Tapping her teeth she sat up. What about the other people who had hit bottom like her and MR ZADROOZNY? To hell with her friends who were too busy doing something cool. She would throw a party for non-cool people. Like MR ZADROOZNY. Like herself. Zed tormented a dream mouse and then disgruntled, woke up. Katie ignored him.

The invitation template and mailing list hummed to life. A quick delete of RSVP and addition of *Pot Luck*. Flipping to the back of the phone book included in her rent, Katie started with Florence Za...

"The people at the end," she told Zed. More needles fell off the tree as she typed. Seeing her at work, Zed jumped up and strolled across her computer keys. He left welts when she pushed him off. Two hours later Katie jogged down to the convenience store and dropped 51 envelopes in the mailbox. MR ZADROOZNY glared at her through the window.

And then the day came. With slightly shaking fingers, Katie lit a couple of festive candles, fiddled with the lights, and rearranged plastic cups and napkins. 7:55...8:00...8:04... "Zed," she wailed, "what if nobody comes! What if even the end of the alphabet rejects me?" Zed waved his tail and wandered across the table in search of something worth eating. "None of the food is here yet," Katie told him.

And then the bell rang. Katie froze and then when the second knock came, sprinted for the door. She pulled it open to a young man holding a package of store-bought cupcakes. "Zach...I need help!" came from down the hall. He thrust the cupcakes into Katie's hands and dashed down the corridor where a young woman wrestled with a stroller.

"Hi Katie!" she called. They got the buggy under control, she grinned, and then her smile faded. "You aren't Katie," she accused. "You don't have a baby!"

"I have a cat..."

The woman fished out the invitation, looked at it and looked at her. "I thought you were Katie from our Lamaze class."

"No, Katie Zeferelli." She pointed at the flickering candles. "I'm having a Christmas party for the end of the alphabet." No question, she realized. She'd fallen over the edge and was seriously crazy.

Zach stuck out his hand. "Zach Zorzi. This is Patti and Kaeden."

Just as the Zorzis were getting a start on the cupcakes, the doorbell chimed again…and again. Zanon…Zander…Zehner…Zenhuang….Zumwalt…Zyback…Zamora…Zymanski…and finally Mr. ZADROOZNY gripping a huge steaming casserole, with a tiny Asian woman in a nurse's scrubs beside him holding out a bottle of wine.

"You?' Mr. ZADROOZNY muttered. "I brought boeuf bourguignon," his face folded and molded into a smile. Sort of.

"Florence Za," the nurse said. "Thank you…thank you for inviting me."

They were all lonely, or curious, or thinking she was someone else, Katie realized. And they all thought she was crazy… but the food was so good. Vietnamese, South American, German, plus a lot of storebought cheese and vegetable trays. Wine flowed. So did conversation among the nurse, convenience store clerk, office manager, electrician, teacher, construction worker, unemployed, and wannabes.

And a few were even cool – like George Zehner a producer for a new TV show. He coaxed Zed from the closet and while the cat purred in his arms and the rest of the guests toasted the season, he offered Katie a job as a goofy best friend on his new series.

It was long past one when Mr. ZADROOZNY left with Florence Za and the others drifted to their homes.

"Merry Christmas," Katie told Zed. He fluffed his fur and plunked onto her pillow. Leaning back against the spare, with "Joy to the World" playing on the TV's crackling fire, Katie texted all her friends about the amazing party they'd missed and her very cool new job.

Christmas Lights

My father loved Christmas – the music, the food, the family and above all, the lights. Our decorations were the talk of the neighborhood. Every window and door, every bush and tree was outlined in brilliant green lights. Three of the neighbors got into the spirit and outlined their houses in red, blue and white respectively. My dad added wooden figures of candles, a choirmaster and choirboys, and then piped out Christmas music that floated through the bare trees and across the Toronto snow.

And at a time when Christmas lights were not particularly showpieces, our stodgy street became a Christmas destination. Cars would growl slowly past. People would stand on the sidewalk, heads turning in pleasure, and my father would go outside and chat, welcoming them all.

My mom and dad grew up on the prairies, facing the world during the Depression. My Dad was the banker who fought with head office to help farmers keep their land; my mother's family ran a general store. She told me about the men who would come in and cry because they had no money left to buy food for their families. Her parents gave them credit anyway and the debts to their wholesalers ate away their own chances of future financial security. My father's home went for taxes when his father died. My grandmother was still teaching in a remote corner of Manitoba in her 70s because, despite years of hard work, they had nothing back.

But they knew Christmas. They knew the joy of gathering family around because life is uncertain and hard; they knew that a Christmas gift worth little, or maybe only a rare orange in a stocking, was what Christmas was about. They knew that the old

14

songs, sung again decade after decade, are the hymns of survival and all that is good about being human. They celebrated with everyone, including their Jewish friends. To them, Christmas was about the open happiness of joy and sharing.

As a cranky teen, I remember lying on my parents' bed beside the green-glowing window, hearing the richness of Nat King Cole's voice calling, "Joy to the world!" and feeling the ease in my angsty soul that only love and generosity can bring.

And now once again, where despite the clever twists of words and policy, we are living in a world where war and destruction are ravaging, hatred and meanness are walking, and contentment and hope are corroding. Many of us are afraid, angry and helpless. We are watching as good people lose their land, men cry because they cannot feed their families, and the number of people who need help are more than we can count.

We are within a cruel time in history.

But, within history, we have our answers and our hope. *This little light of mine, I'm going to let it shine…*

We have the ringing demand, that we offer *Peace on earth, good will towards men.*

And I believe, as my mother and father did, that every Christmas light is a promise of goodness, hope, and generosity towards all. Every twinkling tree and glowing string hanging on a garage gutter is a promise to ourselves and to our shared future. A moment of beauty and peace before we take up the struggle again. A chance to breathe, to remember that our parents, grandparents, and great-grandparents fought for fragile peace and goodwill as well. They too, lit candles and strung lights against the dark nights.

All my family, all my people stretching back over years, hope that every light brings great joy to your life and future.

Happy Christmas!

Christmas Lights ©2018 Susan Brown

Peace on Earth

Jason glanced surreptitiously into the burnished brass of the elevator wall as the lift rose to the top floor. His golden image reflected the carefully chosen tie and the hand-tailored suit on the form he toned every morning at 4:30 in his private gym. His execs stood behind him respectfully, silently. Other than a carefully chosen joke on first meeting each day, they would not speak until he did.

It was only a couple of weeks until Christmas, but the next task was to approve the perfectly crafted ads that would launch their next big campaign. Jason was confident they would be excellent. His staff was well-paid, well-benefited (it made good business sense for staff to be happy) and extremely competent. So everything was all tickety-boo as his grandmother used to say.

Now where did that come from? His Nana had been dead for at least twenty-five years. But unbidden, underscored by the tasteful Christmas instrumentals cranked out by the elevator, he remembered her flour-powdered sweater as she taught him to bake cookies – and the scent of her; sweet and chocolate.

The elevator slid to its stop, and Jason exited through the golden doors. From somewhere came a snatch of the holiday carol, "Peace on Earth, Good will towards men…"

A flick of his eyebrow, and Donna murmured, "I'll look after it…"

She separated herself from the pack and a moment later the non-PC music cut off, mid-lyric.

His grandmother used to blast Christmas music, Jason remembered. Maybe in his office, alone, he could play it softly. His grandmother had stated acerbically that it wasn't much of a gentleman, or a Christian either, who put his own preferences ahead of the comfort of others.

In the conference room, the ad team presented the top choices for the new campaign. There would be eight TV promos – each honed for its target audience. Two of them showed a white, nuclear family ecstatically using their product. Two more showed another, similar family in public, also extolling their product. One showed two white friends practically having an orgasm while they talked about it. There were two more ads, virtually identical, using only black actors.

Jason was bored silly. His highly disciplined mind seemed to have uncharacteristically fixated on peace on earth and his Nana's cookies. A nearly forgotten memory surged up – going with her once to a charitable mission to add their cookies to the bare bones Christmas dinner being prepared for the poor.

There had been Christmas music then too.

He had a sudden, vivid memory of a thin, dark-mustached man with ragged clothes and an accent so thick his words were unintelligible. He had smelled of something pungent and nasty.

Jason relived that jolt of terror as the man bore down on him. Different. Terrible… his feeling of something dark and horribly alien coming too close, threatening him.

The smell, the dark bobbing head…his Nana not *noticing*… "*Tank, tank oo,*" the man growled again and again.

Thanks…thank you, adult Jason suddenly interpreted. And his grandmother had smiled at the terrifying man, while Jason hid behind her.

Thank you…

Jason looked again at the playing ads.

"What do you think, sir?" his advertising VP asked confidently.

"Where are they?" Jason demanded. "Where are the differences?"

"Sir?"

He remembered a little boy, terrified because everything he had seen before had been the same. He remembered the nightmares of the shabby, dark man who had only tried to say thank you for a kindness.

He stood up. "Different," he told the execs. "I want all the differences celebrated. Our company's customers aren't a single flavor and they don't have a single look. Make it happen."

As he walked back to his office, the rebel in the crowd was replaying, "Peace on Earth, Good will towards men."

And Jason was sure he could smell the sweetness of his grandmother's cookies once again.

Boxing Day

In Canada where I grew up, Boxing Day is a holiday. The source of the holiday apparently comes either from, you spent all day in church on Christmas and then on the next day you opened your gift boxes, or the day after Christmas you gave gifts to your staff or the alms box in the church was opened to help the poor.

Whatever.

Boxing Day was always my mother's favorite holiday. After the frantic chaos of Christmas, the rushing about to get those last perfect gifts, the late-night wrapping, the too-early rising, and then the preparation of a feast for all the relatives, to her Boxing Day was like a dream vacation in the Bahamas. Nothing had to be accomplished, there were enough leftovers to feed half the city, and the kids had plenty of new toys and books to keep them busy and out of her hair.

Sometimes the neighbors dropped in with a small gift and the expectation of a glass of good scotch and a plateful of Christmas baking. Even as a kid, I remember the smells, the calm after the storm, the unchecked raids on the refrigerator for my favorite foods. All the stores were closed so there was nowhere to go. Adults and children alike lounged around, reading, chatting, or perhaps going outside for a cheerful snowball fight.

Nothing else in my memory quite compares to that day-long languor of more than enough.

And so I am going to try and officially reinstitute Boxing Day in my life. Some of my family has to work (this is NOT a civilized country), but I will not get in my car to run errands or look after anything. Instead, I'll hang out in my pyjamas, eat leftovers, savor a few too many Christmas cookies, read a novel, and try not to be particularly productive.

I may think over Christmas, think about how the gifts I gave and received are the tangible expression of the love within my family, sip a glass of good scotch (you are so welcome to drop by!) and start mulling over the year past and the year to come. I will remember, savor, and anticipate the good things in my life.

And so, if you can't come by for drinks and treats, I send you my wishes for a day of peace and comfort, a few quiet moments to drop out of the hectic world, and an open door to experience all the blessings of past, present and future.

Here's to you!

We Need a Little Christmas

Torri was between students when the phone call came from her niece.

"I'm sorry, Aunt Torri," Anne sounded like she was trying not to cry. "Josh has to take an extra shift – and the storm is closing off the roads through the pass…we won't make it in time for Christmas."

Torri fought back the emotions that were choking her. It wasn't the first Christmas since her husband, Sam, had died, but somehow this Christmas with all the political terrors creeping into every nook and cranny of life, had made fighting despair harder than ever before. And Anne, Josh and their two pre-schoolers were the only family she had left.

She said all the right things to Anne and hung up the phone. Fighting back gasps, Torri clenched her fists until her knuckles whitened and her fingernails dug into her palms. She wouldn't give in to this. Sam would be disappointed if she gave in. Wouldn't happen. No one would see her misery. Christmas was just another day. She'd have the good coffee in the morning, watch some TV shows that fell into the guilty pleasure category, then…

"Hey Torri," Linda stuck her head in the door, "the cookie exchange is in ten in the staff room. And that little shit, Devon, is waiting to see you again."

"Okay, right," Torri said and forced a smile. "Take my cookies, will you? And maybe make up a box for me, please? Devon might take some time."

She fumbled around for the tin of old-fashioned shortbread she'd made. Sam's mother had taught her the way her own grandmother had taught her years before. She imagined the tradition went back decades if not centuries. All in the handling…

Stop Torri, she scolded herself. *Get a grip. Being alone for Christmas isn't the end of the world…other people have it worse…*

A party. She could have a party…

Not two days before the holiday, she realized with desperation. *Nothing can fix this one, Torri.*

She sat a moment longer, did some deep breathing, then pulled up Devon's file. Hardly a week went by without the fifteen-year-old being in her or the principal's office. Always back-talking. Always razzing other kids. Always doing whatever would irritate the teachers the most. He really was a little shit.

Torri went into the hallway where Devon was lounging, feet sprawled out. He stared with an insolent smile that felt like he really wanted to stick a pencil into her.

"Come on in," she invited. "Let's talk."

When he had draped himself into the chair in front of her desk, and resumed his hard stare, she smiled somehow. "So, Devon, what is it this time?"

He shrugged. "Coach Dick has it in for me."

Torri took a breath. "And did Coach Richards have a reason

to have it in for you today?"

Devon shrugged again, but a flicker of bitter amusement crossed his face before his expression returned to disdainful stone. "Maybe," he muttered.

"Want to give me some details?"

"No."

"I'm missing my cookie party for this," Torri snapped, and then couldn't believe she'd said that. Like she cared about a dozen Christmas cookies. Like it was more important than the boy in front of her.

She dropped her head in her hands. "I'm sorry," she said. "I'm really sorry, Devon." She wouldn't cry. She wouldn't.

She was sobbing.

And then, she felt Devon's hand, awkwardly patting her shoulder. "I'm sorry, Ms. Mac," he stammered. "I didn't mean to make you cry...you're always nice...I was just so mad."

"Oh, Devon," Torri grabbed one of the tissues placed for students and mopped her face.

"You got mascara all over your cheeks," he told her. She had to laugh and mop some more.

"You didn't make me cry, Devon," she said. "My Christmas just went to hell, and with my husband...you know...I'm going to be alone and I'm acting like a baby about it."

"No you ain't," he muttered. "My stepdad split so it's me and my mom and the kids."

"The kids?"

"The three little ones. There won't be no Christmas at our place. If he doesn't come through with child support in January, there won't even be a place to live."

Torri and Devon slumped in their chairs.

Duty called. Torri roused herself and tried to think. "There are some agencies I can call that will make sure your family gets toys for the kids and a Christmas dinner."

Devon gestured angrily. "Charity. Screw that. I got to earn some money. And that damn coach telling me in front of all my

23

friends that I need to man up in class or I won't amount to anything. And all the while he's sitting there stuffing his face. So I grabbed his sushi wrap and threw it at him."

Torri nodded. She remembered a few infuriating interactions with Coach Richards – she'd been tempted to call him Coach Dick herself.

The two of them stared out the window. Snow was falling thick and fast. It was just about certain that school would be cancelled for snow for the last couple of days before the holiday. Now she'd have nothing to do and nowhere to go for even more days. And she would have to shovel out her long driveway. Torri sighed then looked at the lanky teen before her.

"Devon, would you be willing to help me out by shoveling my driveway and sidewalk? My house is easy to get to by bus, and I'll pay you. I could really use the help…I have trouble doing it all myself…"

Devon eyed her, frowning. His hands convulsed on the arms of the chair. "No charity," he snapped.

"Not a chance," Torri told him. "I can't do it and there's supposed to be a lot of snow over the next couple of weeks."

Devon eyed her suspiciously, then nodded. "What time?"

"When can you come?"

"I'll be there an hour after school. Got to check if it's okay with my mom."

Torri scribbled her address and cell phone number on a stickie note and handed it to him. "See you then."

Torri spent the rest of the afternoon watching snow drift by her window, making phone calls to parents and agencies, and checking in with students facing a tough holiday season.

Tougher than me, she chanted in her mind. *They're only kids and they have it tougher than me. And it's Christmas…*

Devon was waiting when she got home, bundled in a coat that was too big for him, no gloves. While he looked around her disorganized garage for a shovel, Torri dug into her hall closet for a warm pair of gloves that had been Sam's.

"You can't work if your hands freeze," she told Devon. "I expect a good job done here."

"Yeah, sure," Devon muttered, then he headed down to the foot of the property.

Torri watched him in the gathering dusk, his arms moving rhythmically as he shoveled the heavy snow from her driveway, then the sidewalk, then her front steps. When he was done, he knocked on the door.

"Hot chocolate?"

"No, I got to go. My mom has to go to work and I have to babysit."

She handed him the money; he pocketed it and turned to go.

"Devon, I've got more work around here that needs doing… any chance you would have some time over the next few days to help me out?"

He scowled. "Yeah. I'll come by tomorrow morning, if you want."

"I want."

When he had disappeared, Torri sat down in her empty living room. She had intended to decorate tonight, but it hardly seemed worthwhile now. The box of stockings, all ready to be hung, sat to one side of the fireplace. The artificial tree twinkled, but she hadn't hung any ornaments. She had been waiting to do it with Anne, Josh and the boys. Her presents for the family were unwrapped, sitting in bags in her bedroom.

Even the outside lights were still untouched in their totes brought up from the basement. Josh had offered to put up the lights when they arrived.

"Better late than never," Anne had observed merrily the week before. The week before the storm cancelled their time together.

"There will be other Christmases," Torri told herself. But she wanted to take the boxes and throw them in the garbage. There

25

might be other Christmases, but she was in the middle of this one.

"Oh stop it!" She ordered herself.

Angrily, she hung ornaments, slammed snow globes onto tables, and wished the window decorations would fall and shatter. When the room was done, she turned out the light, and went to bed.

Devon was at her door before she'd had her second cup of coffee. And with him, he had three kids, a girl and two twin boys ranging in ages from about six to eight.

"My mom got a second shift and we need the money," he told Torri as though she had already yelled at him. "They won't be trouble. What do you need done?"

Torri eyed the kids dubiously. She didn't do small kids. They seemed to always need bathroom help, or noses wiped or zippers fixed. She infinitely preferred the high schoolers' snarky comments and life-altering stupidity. That seemed clearer to her than the physical maintenance needed for younger kids.

"So, do you want me to do anything or not?" Devon demanded. "Shut up, you," he snapped at one of the silent boys.

The kid poked him and Devon flickered a smile.

Torri smiled too. "There are a bunch of branches in the back yard that came down in the last windstorm. I need them collected, broken up, and put in the yard waste."

Like a peeping Tom, she watched from the kitchen window as Devon got the young ones picking up the small sticks under the snow-free shadow of the pines. He cut and broke the bigger branches, then with a quick look around, laughed and chased the little girl until she screamed with giggles.

The boys flexed their muscles to impress their big brother. Torri could hear his admiring comments even though the twins' jackets hid their biceps. He kept them working and playing for nearly two hours.

Then Torri called them into the house. "The kids probably need to go to the bathroom," she told Devon before he could argue. "And I'm not letting anyone get pneumonia."

He glared as she dished up hot chocolate and stuck candy canes in for stir sticks.

Devon stood and drank the hot chocolate, clearly uncomfortable. The kids had no qualms. They settled around her kitchen table, drank the hot chocolate, and chattered about her decorations and their own little tree with the stockings hung on pins on the wall.

"I'm a girl," Lavvie told her, "and I'm almost seven."

"I would like more hot chocolate, please," Davy whispered.

"No," Devon snapped. "That's enough. We have work to do still."

Silently, the three slid off their chairs. Freddy's lip was quivering. "'s cold," he said.

"Don't matter," Devon said.

"Actually," Torri interrupted. " I need to make some cookies…for my great-nephews who are coming…soon. Is there any chance you three could help me?"

Their eyes lit up and they turned beseechingly to Devon. He scowled. "We did all the branches. Anything else, or should I take them home?"

And suddenly Torri desperately didn't want the children to go home. Didn't want the house to be silent and empty. She looked around frantically, and her eyes fell on the Christmas lights that Josh had not arrived in time to put up.

"Devon, my niece's husband was going to put up my Christmas lights, but they're snowed in on the other side of the pass. Could you do it for me?"

A spark flashed in Devon's eyes. "I can do lights," he muttered. "And you three behave yourself or else!" Davy just giggled. Freddy stuck his finger in his mug and grinning, scooped out the last of the chocolate.

"What kind of cookies?" Lavvie breathed.

After that, Torri only glanced out the window a few times. Baking with three kids was like creating a flour storm in her kitchen. She showed them how to make shortbread; they decorated sugar cookies; they even made fudge. Torri put on Christmas music and found herself singing and laughing with the kids.

Devon came in, stamping his feet, cheeks flushed with cold. "Come take a look," he said shyly.

They all bundled and trooped outside. The snow had stopped falling but the blanket of white reflected the lights' glow.

"Is it okay?" Devon asked. Torri caught a hint of nervous quiver in his voice.

She looked around. Lights wound up her trees, twinkled on bushes, and lit the way up her sidewalk.

It was beautiful.

It was all wrong – like everything else.

"My husband never did it like this," she whispered. Anger surged up her chest and she tightened her fists in her pockets. Her breathing came in harsh gasps and she lowered her head.

A moment passed, then Devon strode forward and started ripping the lights off the bushes.

"No," Torri cried. She ran to him and grabbed his arm. "What are you doing?"

"It's no good," Devon yelled. "So I'll take it apart."

"No you won't! You won't! It's all the Christmas I have. You can't…"

The little ones were crying. She was hanging on Devon's arm. And she was crying.

"No…no…no…Don't take my Christmas…"

At last, Devon's arm relaxed.

"I wouldn't," he said. He hung his head.

Torri sniffed. "Inside, now."

For once Devon didn't fight her. Once again, she put the kettle on for hot chocolate but wasn't surprised when no one seemed to want it.

"The lights are beautiful, Devon," she said. "Since Sam, my husband died, I've tried to do everything the same. And it isn't. It isn't at all. I need a little Christmas. A new Christmas, or maybe one that can't be taken from me."

"No one can take Christmas," Lavvie said. "I wished and wished for Christmas cookies and we got them." She smiled and pointed to the piled plates.

"And Devon wanted lights," Freddy said. "We used to have lights but Mama said we couldn't this year."

"I just wanted hot chocolate with a candy cane." Davy grinned.

Devon shrugged. "I can change the lights," he said. "I did them the way we did before my Dad died and we lost the house. But I can change them."

"They're perfect," Torri said. "I don't want anything you've done changed at all – especially not that beautiful display."

He grinned. "Okay then."

She paid Devon, piled her biggest tin full of cookies for the little ones, and waved them all goodbye.

"Okay if I bring my mom to see the lights tomorrow?" Devon yelled back.

"Of course! We'll have hot chocolate and cookies!" Torri called.

They were all laughing when the kids turned the corner and disappeared.

The house was silent again, so Torri turned on the radio to Christmas music while she cleaned up.

When she awoke Christmas morning, the sun glistened on the snow and the coffee smelled like a miracle as it brewed. Torri simply sat and allowed the perfect morning to seep into her soul.

Christmas had come at last.

R. Todd Fredrickson
Snohomish County, WA

R. Todd Fredrickson is the author of *Brothers of the Sun and Moon,* and a book of short fiction, *A Short Five + 2.* He lives in Snohomish County Washington where he enjoys hiking in the Cascades and getting lost in a good book.

You can contact Todd on Twitter at @riverskykomish, or through the Writers Cooperative of the Pacific Northwest website: writers-coop.com.

Holiday Pearl

Holiday Pearl

A picture of my dad's father appeared on the family social media site recently. He is wearing a white button up shirt with a skinny black tie and a mustard color sweater. His flat top hair is darker than I remember, and in need of a comb. Hanging around his neck is the leather strap to his 35mm camera, which he is holding with one hand just below his chest. He is facing an oval mirror that has a gold frame that makes me think of icing on a cake. The image in the picture is the mirror with his reflection. A slight smile on his face suggests he was amused with what he is doing. An original selfie. He would live just a few more years beyond that time, only in his early 60s' his heart had had enough.

It was 1970. I was 7 years old.

I never really knew my grandfather, or his wife. As many times I visited their watch repair shop in Ballard or stayed the night at their house in North Seattle, the only memories I have are sound bites of a moment in time long gone, but like a 9mm home movie, no sound, just flashes of colors and silent laughter.

My parents had divorced two years earlier. My father's affliction with adult libations had taken its toll. Now my siblings and I were part time guests in a house full of strangers. We knew that they were family, but didn't know their names or even who most of them were related to.

Pearl wore her apron as much as William wore his tie. It was a permanent part of her decor when she was home. The house always had a good smell to it because there was always something going on in her kitchen. The holidays were her favorite time of the year because everyone gathered at her place for the day.

A cigarette hung from her mouth and ice clinked on the sides of a glass of bourbon that she held in one hand as she poked a thermostat into the roast in the oven with the other. She licked the grease from a finger and then looked down at me without saying a word, just pinching my nose before moving on to the other side of the counter where she continued pressing a wood rolling pin over damp dough that would become the top of an apple pie.

Some of the adults sat at the dining room table, grazing on nuts, sipping their booze and telling their stories. Others sat on the couch staring at a game show on the television, now and then making a nonsensical comment. Pearl would step out of the kitchen for a moment, a freshly lit cigarette in one hand and her bourbon held up to her face, as if she was appreciating the smell of the whiskey as well as its effect on the soul. Someone laughed in the living room and she stepped towards that room and looked at the TV, and then towards us, my sisters and brother. We were counting the Christmas gifts and looking for our names on the tags.

The Christmas tree used to reach the ceiling, sprayed with fake snow and covered with large red balls. One year it changed to a shorter tree that was mounted on top of a small table. The aluminum limbs shimmered like pom poms. The red bulbs that decorated the white tree were now on this one, but it only took a few of them.

"Need some help, ma?" my father said from his place at the table.

She pinched his nose like she did mine, waved a hand at him and then returned to her kitchen without a word.

The house was built in the 1940's. Small, but solid. The living room was separated from the dining room and the dining room from the kitchen with arched entries. If nobody was sitting at the table I could stand at the television and look all the way through to the back door. In later years I was told about how William had devised a wood rail track under the house and used 5-gallon buckets on a cart to dig out the basement. The stairs into the basement were in the kitchen, with steep long steps. When it was completed there was enough room for a work bench, drill press and band saw. The only window was where a vent in the foundation had been converted with a small glass pane. I never witnessed William down there. Or saw any of his completed projects. My only memory of him was just him passing through from one room to the other, or at his shop in Ballard, where he'd hand us a sucker and then shoo us along.

The dining room table was dark oak, almost black, that had enough chairs for 6 people. They added a few extra chairs when the adult count went beyond that. The kids got to eat their meal on TV trays, while watching TV. Most occasions the programs were benign, not oriented towards our attention.

Besides myself and my siblings there are two cousins, the kids belonging to my father's sister. They were a few years older than my brother, who was 4 years older than me. They didn't talk any more than the adults.

"Good gravy, ma," my father said from the far side of the table. Everyone at the table agreed and then pointed out what else satisfied their taste buds.

"Have another serving," Pearl said, "but save some room for pie and ice cream."

After dinner we piled onto the floor for the gift exchange. The cousins kept their seats on the couch and opened their gifts slowly and then provided a gracious gratitude. The four of us opened ours with a torrent and then were sent to the back yard, out of the way.

When William had his heart attack he was standing in the driveway next to his car, waiting on Pearl. The holidays weren't the same after that day. Neither was Pearl. She spent her remaining years sitting at the dining room table. The TV guide in front of her. An ashtray next to a coffee mug, which was switched with a glass of bourbon in the afternoon.

I was in the Army stationed overseas on the Sinai Peninsula when a call came in from the Red Cross. They patched through my mother who told me Pearl had moved on. Cancer. I thought about how quietly she had battled the illness. It really wasn't any different than how she had lived her life, and then eventually departed. On her own terms and with grace.

Stephanie Larkin
Pacific Northwest

Stephanie Larkin's nonfiction books (*Resettled, Displaced: A Memoir,* and *Grief Country*) touch upon topics as diverse as refugees, Alzheimer's, cancer, stepfamilies, grief, and overcoming life's challenges. She also writes poetry and short stories. She lives in the Pacific Northwest and enjoys traveling in her spare time.
stephlarkinauthor.com

The Gift

The Gift

The opening notes of singer Mariah Carey's iconic classic, "All I Want For Christmas Is You," were just starting to stream from the radio as Molly parked her car outside her cousin's house.

"Yeah, I don't need to hear *that* song," Molly muttered to herself as she turned off the ignition. She reached up and twisted the rearview mirror to the left so she could freshen her lipstick and smooth her hair, then grabbed the holiday wine bag that held a bottle of five-year-old Pinot Noir, her hostess gift. She hesitated as she reached for the driver's side door handle. It wasn't too late to change her mind. After all, that's what all the literature said, right? *You have the right to celebrate or not celebrate the holidays. No one else can tell you how to handle your grief during this difficult time.* For a moment she stared straight ahead, trying to be "mindful" of her surroundings, an exercise she had learned in a widows' support group. Through the windshield she noted the barren deciduous trees that lined the sidewalks, looking forlorn now that their colorful leaves had been stripped away. A few of the neighboring houses boasted large wire displays of reindeer, Santa, and other Christmas favorites in their front yards, biding their time until they could show off their sparkly splendor after dark. "Alright, I'm being *mindful*," Molly said out loud. "I know where I am."

She stepped out into the chilly afternoon air. She was glad she didn't have to walk too far, as she had forgotten her scarf and gloves. She was still forgetting things all the time. At least the stupid things. It was the important things she could not forget. Especially the one important thing.

But now was not the time to think about that. Molly glanced at her cousin's driveway as she walked briskly down the sidewalk. It was a long driveway, but it was already filled with cars. She stepped from the sidewalk onto the walkway that led to the house, her steps slightly less brisk. She could hear Christmas music playing as she approached the front door. Before pressing the doorbell, she took a moment to take a deep breath through her nose and let it fill her lungs, picturing it cleansing the sadness from her body as she breathed out. *Okay, I'm ready for Other People's Christmases again,* she thought as she rang the doorbell.

"Molly!" Her cousin Linda smiled broadly as she enveloped Molly in a hug. "I'm SO glad you made it!" she said. "Come on in!"

Molly stepped inside the small foyer and complimented her cousin's festive holiday décor as her coat was taken and her wine selection was admired. "I'll take this to the kitchen," Linda said, motioning toward the open doorway to the left of the foyer. "Go on in and join everyone in the family room. Besides Gary's family, we invited a few other friends this year. Gary will fix you a drink."

Molly was beginning to feel a few familiar pangs of anxiety as she walked the short distance to the family room. She had hoped her panic attacks were a thing of the past, a "symptom" of widowhood that would be short-lived. *Breathe, just breathe.* She was relieved that the first person she saw was her cousin's adult daughter, Emma. Emma was holding her baby, who would celebrate her first birthday soon. "Oh, Molly, hi!" Emma said with a weary, sleep-deprived-mother smile. "How are you?"

Molly recited her customary response that she was fine as she oohed and aahed over the baby for a few minutes. "I love her little Christmas outfit," she said. "And that candy cane bow in her hair! So cute!" The little girl was indeed adorable. Last Christmas she hadn't yet entered the world, but much of the conversation had centered around her impending birth.

Last year Molly had experienced her first holiday season without Bill, and she had appreciated her cousin's kindness in inviting her to join their family celebration. As an only child, she thought of her cousin Linda as more of a sister than a cousin. Since Molly's parents were deceased, Molly and Bill had spent the past several Christmases with Bill's parents and siblings in California. After Bill died, though, she hadn't heard much from his family. As summer turned to fall and no invitation seemed to be forthcoming, she realized that she was on her own. "Maybe it's just too hard for them to see you," a friend had suggested. "Maybe it brings up grief that they don't want to deal with."

In early December she had received a Christmas card with

a picture of baby Jesus in a manger on the front and a message inside. "We received an invitation from Henry's brother to go to Palm Desert this year," her mother-in-law had written in her spidery handwriting. "We hope you have a nice Christmas with your family." Molly had never met her father-in-law's brother, so of course she couldn't expect to have been invited to join them in Palm Desert. That was the logical way to look at it, right? There was no good, intellectual reason for the piercing stab of pain Molly felt in her heart. She folded the ensuing hurt and disappointment into the fabric of her new life and considered her other options. A few friends had issued invitations, but Molly felt most comfortable accepting her cousin's. After all, Linda and her daughter were "family," the only relatives Molly had who lived in the area.

She hadn't expected it to be easy, but she had still been surprised when Christmas Day turned out to be so excruciating. It wasn't her cousin's fault. It wasn't anyone's fault. No one could have known that every minute of every hour that day would tick by with a voice in her head insistently whispering, "Bill-Bill-Bill-Bill."

When her cousin's mother-in-law admired the beautiful diamond earrings Gary had given Linda, Molly thought about the gifts she would never again receive from her husband. When they had talked about leaving for a skiing trip after Christmas, Molly thought about the trips she would never again take with her husband. When her second cousin Emma complained about being as big as Santa now that she was in her eighth month of pregnancy, Molly thought about the plans she and her husband had made to adopt an older child within the next year or two, since their efforts to get pregnant had been unsuccessful and Molly had reached an age where it seemed

40

riskier to keep trying. At that point Molly had suddenly felt her chest tightening and her heart pounding wildly, and she had abruptly excused herself to go to the bathroom.

When she returned to the party, she had gamely smiled and laughed and offered suggestions for baby names.

"Molly, sorry, but I think I need to change her," Emma was saying, wrinkling her nose in distaste as she bent her head closer to the baby. Molly realized she hadn't been listening to her second cousin for the past few minutes. *Mindfulness!* she admonished herself. *Forget last year. Stay present in the moment!* "Oh, of course," Molly replied. "Go ahead. I'm going to go get that drink from your dad."

Gary greeted her warmly and handed her the requested glass of wine. Molly glanced around. Gary's family members and the handful of guests she didn't recognize seemed to be actively engaged in conversation with one another, so she meandered over to the huge Christmas tree in the corner of the room. Linda's holiday theme this year was a warm red and gold palette, a change from the cool and elegant silver and white she favored last year.

"The tree is beautiful, isn't it?" Hearing this comment, Molly turned towards the woman who had appeared behind her. She wore a friendly smile and a bright red sweater decorated with a small gold Christmas tree brooch.

"Yes, it is. Linda did a wonderful job of decorating this year, as usual." Molly held out her hand. "I'm Molly, Linda's cousin. Are you related to Gary?"

The woman shook Molly's hand and introduced herself. "Nice to meet you. I'm Carol. No, I'm not a relative. I'm a friend of Gary's sister…" She nodded toward the woman wearing a Santa hat who was standing across the room, chatting with

Gary. "She invited me to come." Carol laughed. "So I guess you could say I'm a 'stray.'"

"A stray?" Molly repeated.

"Yeah, you know, someone with nowhere to go for Christmas."

Molly laughed, too. "Well, in that case, I'm a stray, too. I lost my husband a year and a half ago and I don't have any family other than Linda. Well, I thought I did, but it turned out I didn't."

The woman's eyes immediately turned serious. "I'm so sorry," she said, her voice heavy with compassion. "I'm a widow, too."

Molly blinked in surprise. "Oh, my gosh. I'm sorry for your loss, too. I didn't realize there would be another widow here."

"Oh, I doubt your cousin even knows," Carol replied. "In fact, I don't even mention it to anyone any more. It makes people uncomfortable. They don't know what to say, and sometimes they start acting all weird around you."

"I get it," Molly said. She glanced over at a couple of chairs in the corner of the room that had been recently vacated. "Hey, do you want to sit down for a few minutes?"

"I'd love to," Carol replied.

Molly sat down and placed her wine glass on a side table. She wasn't sure how to start the conversation, so she hesitated for a moment.

Thankfully, Carol stepped into the awkward silence. "So Molly," she said, "what's your husband's name?"

Her husband's name? Relief flooded Molly's body. She could feel the tightness in her chest easing. "His name is—was—Bill," she said. "We were married for fifteen years..."

The words poured out of her, random thoughts about Bill, about how kind he was, about the holidays they had spent together, about how he always had flowers waiting on the dining room table when she came downstairs on Christmas morning, about how he always bought extra Christmas cards for her and signed them on behalf of their two dogs, about the Christmas they had flown to Mexico and promptly gotten sick... The minutes flew by, and when she had finally expelled the toxic oxygen of all the pent-up memories and sadness from her lungs, she asked Carol about her own husband, and she had listened intently, finding comfort in the stories of a smart and funny man who had died without warning five years earlier and the woman who had managed to find a way to survive and eventually laugh off the idea of being invited as a "stray" to someone else's Christmas.

"Well, you two seem to be deep in conversation!" Molly looked up to see her cousin Linda standing next to the side table. "I just wanted to let you know that dinner's ready if you want to head into the dining room."

"Thanks! We're coming," Molly replied. She and Carol rose and made their way into the dining room. Soon everyone was seated and compliments about the mouth-watering array of culinary dishes began to fly Linda's way. The menu was basically the same as last year—ham, turkey, traditional side dishes, and a few salads. To Molly, however, it was different from last year. The golden roasted turkey looked more appetizing. The colors of the flowers in the centerpiece seemed brighter. She glanced down at her table setting and wondered if the beautiful china plate in front of her, decorated around the edges with painted poinsettia leaves, was new. Perhaps she just hadn't noticed it last year.

Gary asked those who wanted to do so to bow their heads, then he said grace. Molly recalled briefly how she had bowed her head last year but had nothing to say to God except how could you do this to me. Now she bowed her head and listened as Gary spoke. His words of thankfulness and praise still sounded foreign to her, but she was willing to hear them, at least.

Gary clinked his wine glass with a spoon to get everyone's attention. "Let's have a toast," he said. "To all our friends and family, we're so glad you're here sharing Christmas with us today."

"Hear, hear," his wife Linda echoed, and on the heels of her words, Carol the "stray" spoke up.

"And let's also have a toast to my late husband, Michael, and Molly's husband, Bill. This day cannot go by without remembering what wonderful men they were and how much they loved us."

Tears sprang to Molly's eyes, but they were not tears of sadness. Rather, they were tears of relief and validation and gratitude. Unlike last year, this year her husband had been invited to Christmas dinner. "Thank you," she whispered to Carol when their fellow diners put their glasses down and dug into the holiday feast.

As dusk was beginning to fall, Molly prepared to take her leave. A number of the guests, including Carol, had already left. "Hey, it's snowing!" Gary called out as he stood by the window in the family room. "*What?*" Linda said as she and Molly rushed over to look outside. "It's coming down fast. You'd better drive carefully, Molly."

Molly gathered up her things and said goodbye to her cousin. As she stepped off the porch, she could feel the snowflakes as they gently brushed her face. She imagined them as kisses sent from her husband from up above, and she couldn't help but smile as she got into her car. Pulling the seatbelt across her chest, she noticed the forlorn, barren trees lining the street were now beautifully clothed in a thin layer of fresh snow. The cheerful, twinkling blue lights illuminating a front-yard reindeer caught her attention as she pulled away from the curb. She didn't need to remind herself to be mindful of the beauty around her at that moment.

She hadn't expected much from this day other than maybe a little less pain than last year, but as it turned out, she had received the perfect Christmas gift.

Roland Trenary
Kingston, WA

Born in the first half of the last century, Mr. Trenary maintains that playing the King in his 4th grade's Rumpelstiltskin musical was his undoing. After writing a few books and hundreds of songs, he has yet to disprove this theory.

You can email Roland at: rolandt@iphouse.com

A New Winter Song
Old Old Coat

A New Winter Song

Music soothes the savage breast, it's true.
So
Who would object to you crooning a tune...
Or two?

Wear your trusty, dusty blue jeans
Or some fancy - schmancy   pants,
As the radio   plays songs too slow to sing
Or too fast   for danc-ing.
Yes, with Christmas 'round   the corner,
New Year's Day right smack be-hind,
As you   embrace   the holidays,
Don't you wish   that you   could   find:

    Something that's mem-'rable,
    As unique as a mir-acle?
    An icicle can-ticle?
    A new winter song?

Every frigid   frosty   morning,
When you shovel   off   your walk,
Your Alpaca scarf's   so thick   and soft
It's impos - sible   for   talk-ing.
So your brain hums ancient   chestnuts
For the thirteen-thousandth   time.
But darn it – there   might still   be room
For a melody   sublime:

47

Something that's mem - 'rable,
As unique as a mir - acle?
An icicle can - ticle?
A new   winter   song?

    There's got   to be
    A family - friendly tune   not yet   composed.
    You would love   if one   were written,
    But so far   you   are   un-smitten.

Grab your pads   and pens,   Songwriters!
Bounce those clichés   off   your back.
Comb your minds   for rhymes,   find rhythms
Made for toes   just primed   for tap-ping.
With sufficient   work,   and good luck,
And our prayers,   you'll   do   your   best.
If inspiration   blooms,   "Goodbye"   to bleak,
"Hello"   to blessed,   with

    Something that's mem - 'rable,
    As unique as a mir - acle.
    An icicle can - ticle.
    A new   winter   song!

    Something that's mem - 'rable,
    As unique as a mir - acle.
    An icicle can - ticle.
    A new   winter   song!

Old Old Coat

"I swear, do we n-need money this b-b-bad? Can't we just sell one of the g-grandchildren or s-s-s-something?" In a rickety old lawn chair pushed back against the yellow garage clapboards, Otto's shivering wife, Etta, was bundled in her red parka, its furry hood pulled tight over her stocking-hatted hairdo. Her hand-knit wool scarf was also wrapped thrice around her face, her hands (double-mittened) were folded into her armpits, and her blanketed legs bounced. She had scrunched herself into a roundish shape wedged between the chair arms. It was unseasonably cool this November 6th.

Otto smiled. "Dear, I detect a trace of desperation in your tone. Technically, we've got an hour left. But no one's come along for a while…. I may as well just pack the unsold stuff up. You go on in and get comfortable, why don'tcha? You've been a good sport."

Etta's "YIPPIE!" fogged her glasses. She tipped herself out of the aluminum frame, gave Otto a tiny sideways wave and scuttled across the yard to disappear into the back door of their house.

Otto watched her the whole way. He appreciated her company out here, even if it was for only half an hour. He was chilled himself despite his several extra degrees of warm-bloodedness. In fact, he usually slept with one leg out of the covers all night long while Etta remained curled under two extra blankets.

But she'll be warm soon, and maybe by the time I finish packing up she'll have some soup simmering. One can hope, Otto thought.

As he stared vacantly at the back of their house, lost in this hot soup reverie, a slow scuff of footsteps came down the alley from the other direction. *One last customer then and then that's it.* He swung around.

"Hello Sir," Otto called cheerily to the rotund Gentleman who came steadily closer. "Looking for some bargains? I got 'em! Last sale of the year and I'm closing up, but take your time and look around."

Otto couldn't help himself. He was weary, but still as friendly to this last fellow as he had been to his first treasure hunter four hours earlier. And every one in-between. In fact, he'd enjoyed the whole frigid afternoon, the slow trickle of lookers and buyers. Etta had asked him if the money was worth it, but Otto found more satisfaction in the human interaction and repartee than in any possible pocket full of chilled bills and cold coins. Getting rid of stuff was an added bonus.

"Hmmm? Just looking, methinks," answered The Gentleman.

"Hi. I'm Otto and I'm authorized to entertain any reasonable offers today. I haven't priced anything, so, find something you like and we'll talk. All discounts are applied Otto-matically. Heh, heh, heh."

The Gentleman had already entered the garage and began methodically peering across the cluttered card tables and jury-rigged platforms of planks and ladders, deliberating almost every item and mumbling to himself.

Otto gave him a little quiet time then piped up, "Nothing here I didn't buy myself, back sometime in the near or distant. Some things are actually brand new, you'll notice, but some of them are pretty old too. I'm no youngster, heh, heh."

"Yes, I see. I see." The Gentleman moved carefully, not bumping or tipping or dropping anything.

A set of Santa and Mrs. Claus in painted porcelain piqued his interest, and as he gently held one in each hand, up close to the light bulb that hung from the middle of the ceiling, he declared, "My lord, I haven't seen the likes of these since I was… well… maybe when I was first married. I find it unlikely you bought *these* new, Mr. Otto, for I am quite a bit older than even you."

"Oh, those are lovely for sure. I always liked those. And you're right. Truth be told I guess there's old family stuff here and there, mixed in. Like those. I just forgot – no intention to mislead!"

"Of course not, of course not. No misleading."

As The Gentleman turned and set them back carefully, Otto blurted, "Say, I could give you a really good price on the pair. Since you seem to like them somewhat. Huh?"

"Thank you, but, regretfully, I have no place for them anymore. No place. They are lovely though and I'm sure they will find the right home, eventually. Most do." He continued around the perimeter of Otto's trove then paused where some clothing on hangers hung on a piece of pipe. There were only odds and ends. Nothing had sold from this group all day.

The Gentleman cautiously shifted the hangers one by one. The pipe, strung on a rope fastened at the ceiling, began to swing back and forth. Back and forth. Otto hadn't noticed before, but the fellow was shivering in his reddish-brown suitcoat and matching trousers of an unfamiliar fabric With a thin cloth scarf wrapped around his neck and neatly tucked under his lapels, a modest felt hat from an earlier era, and knit gloves displaying a couple bare fingertips, he was at the mercy of this late autumn chill. *Poor fellow.*

Etta's raised voice reached him from down at the house. She had cracked the back door a few inches. "Are you coming in or what, Otto? The bean soup will bubble soon!"

Otto stepped out around the corner of the garage to wave and holler back, "Just a few minutes, Dear." *I wonder what combination from her storehouse of beans she's cobbled together this time?* He mused as he pivoted to return to his customer.

He jumped backwards. The Gentleman was standing right in front of him, his face sort of glowing. Several days' beard-stubble caught the garage bulb's glare like cactus spines catching morning sun. *Yes. Definitely a glow thing happening here.*

And… he was wearing The Coat.

Oh My! Otto had forgotten. How could he have forgotten? The Coat had been his father's from way back, perhaps just after the War. And he had almost lost it, being the last thing left before the new owners had moved into his father's house. He found it in the tiny entryway closet as they were literally going out the front door for the very last time, hustling to the 2 pm closing at the title company. For ten years more it had hung in their own hall closet. He had had quite the conversation with Etta. An argument almost, but, caught in the sale-item-sweep…it was moved to the garage despite Otto's vaguely sentimental objections.

Now, it hung on the shoulders of The Gentleman. He spoke to Otto…

"My new Friend, you do not know me.
I am just another Traveler.
I have been upon this planet for… well…
let's not count the years,
And I've stretched my Time so thin that
now I fear it's almost broken.
Plus, the Elements have spoken:
they desire to freeze my skin."

Was this some sort of confession, or song, or…? Otto was silent.

"Yet, this Garment, like a bearskin,
has appeared on my horizon
To accommodate my person,
granting respite from the wind.
For it's true, West Winds send howlers
that might frighten sturdy bison.
And if I may ask a question:
this Coat hangs for sale, my Friend?"

Otto stood transfixed. Lulled. Dumbfounded. Letting The Gentleman's lilting yet gravelly voice flow over him…

"If a Winter isn't pleasant,
folks don't contemplate a descent
Into Hades for its climate,
though they're told it's more than warm.
No. They claim the Spring is nearing
(and wear icicles like earrings)
For all humans hide short mem'ries
and protest at each New Storm."

That's true enough. I never remember anything anymore…

"Nonetheless, I must confess:
today may be my final quest. And,
Just like any Knight before me,
I'm surprised each dawn of day.
With this Customary Armor
(which will wrap and keep me warmer)
I may live to fight this Wint'ry Battle.
If you give your say."

This is a strange bargaining tactic, thought Otto. But he continued to listen, frozen in place…

"And I need not make inquiry
as to Ownership before me,
For I understand the lineage
such a Royal Shawl might claim.
In fact, you yourself must harbor
such suspicions that may linger –
As to Gallant Warriors Previous.
(But let's not mention names.)"

Well… before my father? I don't…. Was the coat even older?

"If your heart does sense me Worthy
(and you do not need the money)
You must recognize that conjuring
and coinage seldom mix.
So, let Magic be the conduit
to reach and teach: 'Just Do It.'
Let us conjure a solution, Thus.
You shall not be remiss."

Otto's thoughts of soup had drained away; Etta's voice had become a forgotten echo; dusk was settling into the world's corners. *Has a minute passed? An hour? What is he talking about?*

"In the future, too, I promise,
my Demise offers this solace:
I shall pass this cloak for nothing.
Every Right begets a Right.
Any spell we both partake of shall, again,
be what Hope's made of.
Gains or Losses balance in the end,
as Grace gathers the Light."

The Gentleman thrice nodded, spun around and, as Otto blinked, was gone, leaving behind only the yellow glow of the garage bulb and a melodic tinkling, lingering in the chill.

Etta came up behind Otto. She'd wrapped an extra comforter around herself yet shivered. "Silly m-man! Come in for soup! Just c-c-close the garage door and we'll make room for the car tomorrow. Hello? Wake up!"

Otto shook himself within his stupor, his brain foggy. "Yes. No more sales today, I guess."

All gone. All sales final.

He reached in his jacket pocket, squeezed the remote control and turned to shuffle across the yard behind Etta while humming The Gentleman's melody-less tune under his breath.

Linda Jordan
Tulalip, WA

Linda Jordan writes fascinating characters, visionary worlds, and imaginative fiction. She creates both long and short fiction, serious and silly. She believes in the power of healing and transformation, and many of her stories follow those themes. Linda now lives in the rainy wilds of Washington state.

She can be found online at: www.lindajordan.net

The Christmas Mug
The Best Little Christmas Ever
Marta and the Christmas Cat
We Wish You a Merry Christmas

The Christmas Mug

Beatrice sat in the near empty coffee shop across from the hospital, hands wrapped around the paper cup of strong mint tea with honey. It warmed her hands, but the rest of her felt cold and numb. The sound system played jazz which barely kept her awake and annoyed her with its dissonance, all at the same time.

She should have ordered black tea, but her stomach couldn't handle it. The awful burger she'd had at the hospital cafe last night still roiled around in her stomach.

She smoothed her wrinkled jeans. She hadn't been home to change since the ambulance came. This was the first time she'd left the hospital.

Dad was dying. Beatrice had spent the last two years taking care of him, not out of duty, out of love. She'd taken a leave from her high paying tech job and moved back into the house her family had lovingly tended since before her birth. Watching Dad's slow decline in health, she took technical writing jobs and worked at home.

She'd watched his gradual, painful descent into Alzheimer's. For the last few months he'd had no idea who she was and kept calling Beatrice by her older sisters' names, Meredith and Hannah. She'd been able to mostly let that go and not take it personally. She had chosen to take care of him, while her sisters lived in other cities far from Seattle, mostly ignoring her reports on his health.

Until the accident two days ago.

She'd been in the shower. He tried to go up to the second floor of the house and fell, hitting his head on the wood banister.

She'd stayed at the hospital, sleeping on a cot in his room. Feeling terribly guilty until the doctor said, "You do know, he's been rapidly declining for the last six months. There was not much you could do, short of clone yourself. You might have been using the toilet and the same thing could have happened. At worst what you did was speed up his decline by a month or two. At best you shortened the amount of time he will spend in very severe decline, completely unable to relate to the world."

Finally, Beatrice had gotten hold of both her sisters.

"You should come. The doctor says he's not going to recover."

"How long does he have?" Meredith wanted to know.

"A day, maybe two or three. She's not sure."

This morning, Meredith and Hannah had descended on the hospital room and pushed her aside. She replayed the scene in her head, unable to get the antiseptic hospital smell out of her senses.

"You need a break," said Meredith, an attorney in San Francisco.

"You look tired," said Hannah, a fashion magazine editor in New York.

Beatrice had stroked her short hair, trying to make it stay in place. It was sticking up in back, like always. She must look terrible, even though neither of them said that.

So, she gave Dad a hug, not that he acknowledged it. He hadn't been conscious since the fall. Hadn't opened his eyes. The nurse said he probably wouldn't either.

She had said her last words to him long before. Told him she loved him, loved being with him, talking about the history he'd lived.

Beatrice felt a kind of peace that she'd taken leave from work six months before. She didn't regret any of the time spent caring for him, or the lack of a cushy paycheck.

But how was she going to survive the emptiness ahead? For the last several years her life had narrowed down to the two of them. Now, it was just her.

She should go home and sleep, but the hospital coffee this

morning had left her too wired. And it was a bright winter morning. She'd never been good at napping or sleeping during the day.

The last place she wanted to go was home. How could it be a home anymore?

She tapped the Uber app and requested a ride. She'd left her car at home, rode in the ambulance instead.

When the Uber car arrived, Beatrice left the coffee shop and got in. The driver was a chatty young man in his early twenties.

"You want to go to Fremont?" he said. "I just adore Fremont. So many delicious cafes and shops."

"Yes," she said.

"Where in Fremont?" he asked.

"If you just drop me off close to the statue, I've got some errands to run."

"Which statue? Troll, Lenin or Waiting for the Interurban?"

"Interurban."

"Done," he said.

She asked him how he liked driving for Uber. His answer took the rest of the half hour drive from Pill Hill to the Fremont district.

She got out of the car, just across the street from the statue of six people and a dog with a human face waiting under a pergola for a train that would never come again.

She felt relieved to be away from his chattering as the car drove off. It was raining in Fremont.

Beatrice stood under an awning trying to decide where to go. She'd been planning on wandering through some of the little shops and then walking the six blocks home.

The rain continued to pour down, spattering everywhere. Cars drove by fast on the busy street adding to the splashing. She didn't even have a coat or an umbrella, just the Seattle sweatshirt she'd bought at the hospital gift shop.

After calling the ambulance, she'd barely remembered to grab her purse, phone, phone charger and keys. Then turn all the lights in the house off.

She'd spent the two days in the hospital roughing out a draft for a user manual for software that she knew well. On her phone. While watching Dad lie there looking as if sleeping and growing paler each moment. As if writing on her phone wasn't a special kind of hell, doing it in the hospital with a dying loved one just capped the whole thing off. Her brain hurt, her eyes ached and her heart felt shattered.

Beatrice glanced around the wet sidewalk and decided to go inside one of the nearest shops and hope the rain would let up a bit. Maybe she'd even find an umbrella.

She decided Bibi's Bargain Boutique was closest. She sprinted out from under the awning to the next doorway. As she closed the door behind her, tingling bells sounded over the street traffic outside.

The shop was comfortingly warm with a faint smell of incense. Aisles of wood furniture stood in front of her. Off to her right were glass cases filled with jewelry and other precious items. Colored twinkle lights hung from the ceiling and around large pillars. Vintage decorated aluminum Christmas trees filled the window display. Soft classical music played over the sound system.

It took a minute or two for Beatrice to realize Christmas was a week away. She'd forgotten about it with the crisis of Dad's fall. He wouldn't make it till Christmas.

An older woman stood behind the counter. She had dyed orangish hair that looked as difficult to control as Beatrice's.

"Good morning. You look a little damp. I can't believe the rain we're having."

"Yeah, it's pouring out."

"Well, you can dry out in here. I've got the heat ramped up, trying to keep things from mildewing. Nobody wants that."

"Thanks," said Beatrice, nodding and wandering to the right side of the store where there were clothes, kitchen goods, lamps and even a few books.

"Let me know if you need any help."

"I will."

She strolled down aisles of antique dishes, cast iron pots and hand embroidered tablecloths. Some things were worth a lot of money, and marked accordingly. Others were simply a decade or two old and priced low.

The store's contents and displays had a whimsical feel about them. There was a large display of fancy tea pots. Dainty cups and saucers set next to handmade cloth napkins. Mixing bowls, two cake pans, a flour sifter, wooden spoons, glass and metal measuring spoons and cups were all arranged on an oak Hoosier cupboard. Its flour drawer hung open, as if to suggest everything you needed to bake a cake, other than the ingredients, was there for the buying.

She stopped at a display of large mugs, all of them from the past few decades. The one that caught her eye was red with white snowflakes on it. She remembered using the exact same one as a kid. Mom had made hot chocolate for her in just such a mug. The white marshmallows floating in the dark brown chocolatey liquid.

Mom, who'd died when she was five. Beatrice barely remembered what she looked like and those memories only from photographs. Dad had been the one who raised her. Her sisters were in college by the time Mom died.

The last time Beatrice has seen her, Mom had walked her to kindergarten and waved goodbye as the bell rang and Beatrice skipped into her class, happy to be at school. Mom had been walking home when a drunk driver hit her.

Beatrice had dreaded going to school for years, always afraid she'd come home to find her world completely changed and everyone she loved gone.

She picked up the mug and examined it. The red glaze looked like new. She blinked away the tears and took it to the cash register.

"Oh, that's cute. It just came in yesterday," said the woman, ringing her up.

"I had one as a kid," said Beatrice, handing her a debit card.

"Well, Christmas is a time for us to be childlike again," said the woman. "I'm Bibi."

"Beatrice."

"What a lovely name. You know what it means, of course." Bibi handed her the card back and wrapped the mug in old newspaper and a plastic bag.

"I don't actually."

"Bringer of happiness. It was my sister's name."

"Thank you. I could use some happiness right now."

"I thought so. May this mug bring you happiness," said Bibi, handing it to her.

As Beatrice took it, their fingers touched. She felt a surge of energy flow through her, as if a gentle electric current gave her the power to make it through this day and those following.

"Do you need an umbrella?" asked Bibi.

"I do," said Beatrice. "I left mine at home."

"You can borrow one from the umbrella stand by the door. Bring it back next time you're in the neighborhood."

"Thank you," said Beatrice. "I'll do that."

She picked up a cheery purple umbrella with hot pink hearts on it and opened it on the other side of the door.

She walked half a block to the market and bought whole milk, peppermint vegan marshmallows and some fancy hot chocolate mix made from artisan chocolate. As an extra treat she put a bag of star-shaped, frosted gingerbread cookies in the basket.

At home, Beatrice cleaned up the mess, vacuumed the house and got the artificial Christmas tree Dad had always insisted on, out of storage and dragged it into the living room. She put the fragile decorations on while listening to Christmas music. She strung lights throughout the entire house, even Dad's room until the place was filled with light.

She burned bayberry candles to change the scent of the house, which reminded her too much of the hospital.

Then Beatrice set the cocoa, marshmallows, cookies and the mug in the center of the kitchen table almost like a flower display.

She was going to need them.

She made a quick peanut butter and strawberry jam sandwich for herself and ate it. Cleaned herself up and changed her clothes. Then got in her car and returned to the hospital.

Her sisters were still in Dad's room, huddled in the corner talking.

"There hasn't been any change," said Meredith to her.

Beatrice sat down by Dad's bed and took his cold hand.

"Hi Dad, I'm back."

"He can't hear you," said Hannah.

"Course he can," said Beatrice. "Ask one of the nurses, they'll tell you."

Dad had been moving his other hand, almost nervously, touching his chin. The nurse had told her this was normal. His breath came in gasps and then for a time there would be no breath at all, then he'd repeat the pattern.

At least he looked peaceful.

"We need to talk about arrangements," said Meredith.

Beatrice looked at her, annoyed. Then she understood. They wanted it to be done, so they could go back home.

"When do you need to leave?" she asked.

"I need to be back on Monday afternoon."

Today was Friday.

She looked at Hannah.

"Monday morning."

Beatrice nodded. "I've got everything covered. Funeral arrangements were made decades ago when Mom died. It's all paid for."

"What about the will?" asked Meredith.

"His lawyer has it."

"Are you going to be all right, with no job?" asked Hannah.

"I have a job, several different contracts, actually. I never stopped working. Just took leave from the one job so I could work at home."

"Oh," said Hannah, looking confused. "I thought you weren't working at all. Just taking care of Dad."

"That was on the side. I've been doing technical writing."

Meredith said, "Is that as interesting or lucrative as creating software?"

"No, but it's good enough. I wanted to spend the time with Dad. It allowed me to do that."

Doctor Schüller came by for her rounds and talked to them.

Beatrice mostly tuned her out as Meredith peppered the doctor with questions that Beatrice had already asked.

She watched Dad as he stopped breathing again. His other hand lay by his side, still. She felt as if his soul was sliding out of his body, freed from the burden. He didn't breathe again.

Eventually, Meredith ran out of questions. The doctor moved to examine Dad and looked at Beatrice. Doctor Schüller nodded at her as if to tell Beatrice what she already knew and Beatrice nodded back.

"He's gone," said the doctor to Meredith and Hannah.

Beatrice felt the wall of grief inside threaten to overwhelm her and pushed it back down. She'd grieve when she was alone, not around strangers. They might be her sisters, but they felt like strangers.

The next two days went by in a rush. Meredith and Hannah planned the funeral. All Beatrice did was show up. When she wasn't at their hotel, she slept.

Hannah and Meredith wanted to take her out to dinner. Beatrice lied, saying she had an immovable deadline and had already lost three days; that she knew they'd accept without arguing. She saw them at the funeral on Sunday and went home that night to an empty house.

She turned all the Christmas lights on and lit a fire in the wood stove. It was chilly in the house. She put some classical Christmas music on the old stereo.

Then she took her new mug, washed and filled it with milk and put it in the microwave. Then stirred in the cocoa mix. Topping it with the marshmallows, she got a plate of cookies and took the food into the living room and set it on the coffee table.

She opened the door of the wood stove so she could watch the flames dance and sat on a large pillow by the roaring fire, drinking hot chocolate and crying, her grief flooding out. Heartache at the loss of her dad, pain at the loss of her mom. Her family was gone, most of them long ago. The sisters, she barely knew and didn't care to, both long lost.

Hours later, she had cried out as much sadness as possible. There would be more tomorrow. And the next day.

She ate a gingerbread cookie and washed it down with cold hot chocolate. She cradled the mug in her hands, as if holding on to something. A promise of the future.

What was it that Mom used to tell her? "Tomorrow will be better. You can start a new life then."

And she would.

The Best Little Christmas Ever

It all started when Schewandalii, Schew for short, stopped in at a grungy looking convenience store on his way home from work. It was a long drive to and from Santa Barbara, so the Setagean Consulate hired a car service for some of its employees. Schew was lucky enough to qualify. The human driver sat in the car while Schew went inside for a giant grape sloppee and picked up a newspaper.

The cashier stared at him openly. Some humans were like that. They hadn't seen enough aliens or perhaps they resented the contract the world governments had made with the Unity, the group of alien governments. Many humans, he knew, saw it as a take over. His people, from Setagea, saw it as a sharing of the universe's resources. Earth was not meant just for humans alone.

He slurped the drink through his mouth, feeling the sugar buzz through his twelve blue feelers. Schew sighed with pleasure. Earth did have some wonderful things.

He ambled back out to the car and stretched his arm to twice the normal length to get his drink in the cup holder, then rolled into the car using his five legs, and pulled the door closed.

"Home, James," he said, mimicking something he'd heard in a silly old movie. Although this driver's name was Jonathon.

The driver didn't laugh. Humans had no sense of humor.

He flipped open the newspaper. Earthling's still insisted on using them. Even in this day and age. Simply amazing. He liked the scent of the hemp paper. The texture was pleasing, as well. His associates at the Consulate had accused him of going native. It was partly true. He loved everything, well almost everything, about Earth. He wasn't crazy about the smog, but he could live with it.

Paging through the newspaper, he was struck by all the Christmas ads. Only seven more shopping days, they said. His family had never celebrated Christmas, they'd only watched from afar, marveling at how the holiday had sprung up and been translated through various myths and religious traditions, then by commerce. Religion was nonexistent on their own planet, so there were no religious holidays. Schew and his family had been on Earth for ten years. They'd come one year after the Unity treaty had been signed.

It was time, then. He'd always wanted to, but life was always so busy. He'd have to find out what was involved in Christmas. Shopping for gifts seemed to be a major activity. What fun that would be.

He loved shopping. And gifts.

But Christmas was a huge commitment. Would the podlings go for it? And Mabel, what would Mabel think? His feelers wilted, just a little.

The driver pulled into the driveway at Schew's house. It was a modest 1980's vintage rambler. Schew and his podlet, Mabel, had fallen in love with it at first sight. They moved in and immediately painted it Cotton Candy Pink with Screaming Orange Sunset trim. Just looking at the house made him feel happy. That was good after the day's work he'd had.

Schew got out of the car as the driver opened the door. He grabbed the newspaper and the half finished sloppee and moved towards the house, but not before noticing the driver's look of disgust. After which the man whipped out a towel and began to dry off the back seat of the car with exaggerated motions. Earth simply wasn't prepared for dealing with aliens. On other Unity planets, moisture absorbing and obliterating covers were used for seating areas. Humans. Sometimes they were brilliant, sometimes mystifying.

He opened the front door of the house and was nearly bowled over by Mabel.

"Sloppee, you brought home a sloppee," she said, grabbing it and bouncing down the hallway.

He laughed, a deep, gurgling laugh, which filled him with desire. He dropped the damp newspaper on the entryway table and chased her down the hall.

She went through the kitchen and out onto the back patio, made of concrete that they'd painted Key Lime Green. By the time he caught up with her, she'd finished the sloppee and had put the cup down.

"Ooooh," she said, "that felt so good."

He politely waited until the sugar had made its way through her feelers, then he pounced. She bounced across the patio, giggling, as she allowed him to catch her. Their feelers entwined, along with their arms and legs. He caught the sugar buzz from her feelers and deep behind it felt her reaching out to him. She touched him as deeply as he touched her. Sensations of fullness, skin against skin stroking each other and tickling nerve endings filled him with joy. He could even taste the grapeness.

They lay entwined for some time, basking in the sun on the slippery concrete, their slime forming a pool around them. He stroked the skin closest to her eyes, gazing at her. They'd had four sets of podlings together and he still loved her like the day she'd been born. She was amazing.

Finally, they separated and she stood and said, "Let's go for a swim."

"Okay."

They leapt into the pool, bobbing around in the murky water, searching for mosquito larvae and algae clumps until satisfied. Then they sat on the edge in the sun. That's when he brought up his crazy idea.

"I think we should celebrate Christmas this year."

"Christmas! Whatever for?" she asked.

He could tell from her accent that she'd been watching the BBC Channel again.

"Because, why not? We never have. It would be fun. We could do all the Christmasy things and the podlings would have a great time. And there's gifts."

"Gifts. From who?" she asked, scrunching up her mouth.

"I'm not sure. But I think everyone buys everyone else gifts."

"I don't know," she said. "Everyone always complains about Christmas. How much work it is. How they don't know what to get Aunt Kalissi. That sort of thing."

"Yet they turn around and do the same thing the very next year. It must be fun. And I do like all the lights."

"Ooooh," she said. "That's right. The lights. I do adore all the neighbor's lights every year. Our cute little house would look even cuter with lights on it."

"And they're selling silvery lighted Christmas trees. There was an ad in the paper. Wouldn't that be nice in our living room?"

She twisted a feeler between her long articulated fingers. "What exactly is the purpose of a Christmas Tree? I've never really understood."

"I don't know. We may have to do some research. But I'd love to have an old fashioned Earth Christmas."

"Okay," she said. "Let's do it. Christmas is on. I'll talk to the neighbors and see what I can find out."

His feelers popped up, despite himself. Mabel never wanted to talk to the neighbors.

By the time their podlings, Two, Four, Six and Nine, got home from school, Schew and Mabel had made a plan.

"We're going to celebrate Christmas this year," he announced.

"Ooooh," squealed Two with excitement. "What's Christmas?"

"I don't wanna," said Four.

Six asked, "Why?" with a sneer.

Nine just shrugged and went to its room.

Mabel turned to Schew and whispered, "Just ignore it. It's going through the change. It'll come around, you'll see."

Schew continued, "Christmas is an Earth holiday that's full of

69

fun. We'll decorate the house and shop for surprise gifts for each other and have a great time.

"Oooh," squealed Two.

"I don't wanna," said Four.

"Why?" asked Six. With a smaller sneer.

"Because we want to have fun!" said Schew. "Now, who wants to go buy Christmas lights with me? We need to get into the Christmas Spirit around here?"

"I wanna go!" shrieked Two.

He knew Two would agree to almost anything. Except ice cream. Two hated ice cream with a passion.

Four shrugged and said, "Okay."

Six said, "Why not?"

"I'm going," said Mabel.

"You coming Nine?" asked Schew, raising his voice.

There was no answer.

Schew went down the hall to its room, turned off the blaring music and asked, "You coming?"

"I've got homework," said Nine.

"Homework. Who cares? This is Christmas. C'mon."

"I suppose," said Nine.

They rolled into the big autovan and Schew programmed in their destination, The Everything Mart. The store where if they didn't carry it, they'd make it for you, right there on the spot. That technology had come from the Cassions. They were brilliant at transforming things.

The six of them walked, rolled, bounced, limped, ambled and slid into the brightly lit store. Schew immediately caught the scent of chocolate in the air. It was even Duveilian chocolate. So not only was the store using sensory stimulus to keep people around, but to get them aroused as well. He and Mabel better be careful. They didn't need more podlings until these four were gone. Room sharing had not worked well with the first two sets.

"There they are," said Mabel, grabbing a shopping cart and pointing to a display of Christmas lights.

They rushed over and began loading lights into the cart and then decided that still wasn't enough, so they got two more carts and filled those as well.

Then in the fourth cart, they put in a box containing a shiny silver and teal Christmas tree, plus boxes and boxes of all sorts of ornaments. Schew especially liked the box containing all sorts of aliens.

Mabel screeched when she found ornaments of her favorite English TV series, a remake of 'Pride and Prejudice'. Two grabbed a box of multicolored ponies. Four wanted spooky ghosts and werewolves. Six picked a box of spaceships. And nine, well nine, as usual, pretended to not be with them. But it did grab a box of musical instrument ornaments.

They decided that was enough decorations for this trip. They'd get more another day. It would take them all night to put these up.

As they ran things through the auto-checkout, Mabel grabbed a container of eggnog from a cooler nearby.

"The neighbors told me about eggnog. We have to drink this while we're decorating," she said, plopping it onto the scanner. "We've got some alcohol at home. At least for the two of us."

When it was all added up, the cost was 2,492.54 Unity Credits. Schew scanned his hand, thinking that was an awful lot for just decorations. They still had gifts to buy and events to go to.

At home, they unloaded the whole mess in the living room and began sorting through which lights would go outside and which inside.

"Let's put the tree up first," said Two.

"We need to put the outside lights up while it's still light out," said Nine.

Schew gazed at the setting sun. Well, at least they'd have Christmas lights to work by if they plugged them in. They chose four hundred strands for outside the house and six hundred for inside. He set Mabel, Two and Four to start work on the inside.

Six and Nine went to help him outside. In the garage, there was a ladder that was tall enough to reach the roofline. It took all three of them to carry it out and set the thing up. Schew looked up at it, his abbleblabble shrinking. He was afraid of heights. He hadn't counted on roof lights as part of celebrating Christmas.

Six and Nine stared at him.

Finally Nine said, "I'll go up."

Nine climbed the ladder stringing the lights along with it. It snapped a glue tab out of the package and attached the tab to the roof, then the light string to the tab. One section down, 399 to go.

They finally finished the outside lights just as the sun was coming up the next morning. The three of them stood in the street admiring their work. The cute little pink and orange house looked stunning, decked out in multicolored lights, twinkling and shifting colors. Schew could hardly wait till after sunset tonight to see what it looked like in the dark. They'd wrapped the palm trees and banana plants as well. And in back, the gazebo over the patio. The whole place looked like a hotel he and Mabel had stayed at for one of their honeymoons. It was on Richter 42. Magical times, yes, magical times.

They managed to get the ladder back into the garage, but they were all feeling shaky. Maybe that was what the eggnog was for.

Inside the house, everything was lit up. There were lights strung everywhere, even the floor. They made a game of it, trying to cross the floor without touching any cords or light bulbs. The tree hung from the ceiling, filled with all the beautiful ornaments.

Their little house looked extraordinary.

Mabel poured eggnog into glasses, adding the rubbing alcohol into his and hers. He drank some and decided it was pretty good tasting stuff.

Two loved it and asked for more, Four hated it, Six thought it was spiff and Nine drank, shrugged and went to its room.

Schew sat back in the lounging chair and said, "So. This is Christmas. I like it so far."

Then he promptly fell asleep. And missed work. He slept all day.

He woke up at dinner time and said, "That eggnog put me out. I think I better save it for the weekend."

Mabel said, "All of you were so tired, poor things. I let you all sleep."

He rubbed his feelers. "Oh, the podlings aren't at school. Good. We need to do more research on Christmas. Find more activities for us to do."

They all sat in front of their screens, except for Nine, who said, "Screens are so old fashioned." It refused to use one, still hoping its demand for an implant would be granted.

Not likely. Schew was an old fashioned Setagean. No reason to ruin a perfectly good body by cutting into it. Some things humans did were fine with him, but not that one.

"All the kids are doing it."

"You're not a kid. You're a podling. You're above all that."

Nine whiffled his feelers about, just short of being insulting. Schew ignored him, just like Mabel had told him to do on those occasions. He'd forgotten what it was like to go through the change. It had been so long. Mabel had been studying up on it. She studied up on everything. Such a good leader, she was. He always felt so proud to be hers.

"There's something called a nativity set," said Four. "I think we need one."

"Okay," said Mabel, tapping her feelers against her bulbous head. Which meant she was adding it to a list.

"We need to watch something called *The Nutcracker*; it's called a ballet," said Two. "What's a ballet?"

"Probably some type of eating competition," said Mabel. "I'll look into that."

Six said, "Someone said we need to go look at vintage stores for decorations."

"Added," said Mabel. "Although I'm not sure what a vintage store is. Or what else we still need for Christmas."

Nine said nothing. It perched on the couch, pretending not to be paying attention.

Schew searched for vintage stores, wondering what sort of wine they sold. The only one he could find nearby had closed an hour ago. Apparently, they didn't cater to their customers. The family would have to go there tomorrow.

"I got tickets for *The Nutcracker*," said Mabel. "It starts in thirty-five minutes. And it'll take us twenty minutes to get there."

"Okay, let's go," said Schew.

There was a flurry of activity ending with all of them settling into the autovan. Mabel programmed in the destination and they were off.

With ten minutes to spare, they arrived at the building. It was an old Earth building with gold painted columns at the entrance and filled with row after row of chairs. Schew looked around and could only see humans. They were the only Off Worlders at the ballet. Interesting.

The place had slippery wood floors and smelled of furniture polish. Which was very tasty.

Suddenly the lights went dim. He wondered if it was a power brown out.

Then in the front of the big room, the curtain rolled up and there were people moving about a huge Christmas tree. Which was on the floor! Imagine that. What a silly place for a tree. If you wanted that, why not just plant one in your yard?

Music filled the air and the story began. Although Schew couldn't really understand it. He still had so much to learn about Earth.

Still, when the ballet was finished, they'd all enjoyed it.

"I never knew humans could move like that," said Mabel, on their way out of the building.

"I liked the costumes," said Two. "I want to wear clothes."

"I liked the house," said Six. "I want to live in that place."

"I liked the food at intermission," said Four.

"I thought the story was interesting," said Schew. "What did you like?" he asked Nine.

"The lights, of course."

After work and school the next day, they all gathered and decided to go to the vintage store that Schew had found.

They piled into the Van and drove across town. Eddie's End of the Line Antiques was in a part of the city, they'd never been in. It was squeezed in between a laundromat, whatever that was, and a used bookstore. The area wasn't as brightly lit as any of the malls.

"Well, this doesn't look promising," said Schew.

"It must have something interesting," said Mabel, wearing her 'trying to be positive' expression, which consisted of twining two feelers together.

"Okay, let's make a game of it. Each of us will go inside and find one present for everyone in the family. You can't look at anyone else while shopping to try to see what they've bought, you have to keep what you're buying hidden from the rest of the family. The gifts are supposed to be a secret."

Nine rolled its eyes.

Six sighed.

Four said, "I don't wanna."

Two said, "I'm too old for games."

Mabel said, "I'm in."

Schew opened the van door and they wandered inside the store. Eddie's was filled floor to ceiling with stuff. The most amazing things he'd ever seen. Schew wandered through the aisles marveling at objects people had made, used and tossed aside. He found so many strange things. Schew finally had to ask a young man, wearing a neat, white shirt, navy colored pants and a badge which read *I'm Abelard - How May I Help You?*, who looked like he worked at the store, what they were. The items turned out to be a candle holder, a red wagon and a pair of television antenna. The names of which didn't make clear what they were used for and the employee couldn't tell him. Schew hadn't a clue what most of the things in the store were, but they certainly were fascinating.

He picked up a bicycle tire pump for Four, not knowing what a bicycle was. Each time Schew found something interesting, he had to ask the young man what it was. Schew found a plastic pony for Two, who loved ponies. Abelard clenched his fists, when trying to explain what it was. A model train set for Six, who loved history. The young man clenched his fists and his face turned red, while trying to explain. A guitar for Nine, who loved music. The man's face wrinkled up and drips of water ran down his face, all while trying to explain as Schew asked question after question. Schew searched and searched a gift for Mabel and was about to give up, when he found a long, flowing piece of fabric in purple, red and flaming orange. It would look and feel fabulous wrapped around her feelers. The young man had disappeared by then. It had taken Schew so long to find the gift. Schew hoped Abelard was all right. Sometime he had that effect on humans, they were overcome by his friendliness.

He smuggled all his things up to the cash register. A large, balding man with a mustache sat on a stool and looked annoyed at having to get up.

"I'd like to buy these and I'll also pay for whatever my family wants."

"Christmas shopping, huh?"

"Yes. It's our first time to celebrate it and we're having so much fun."

"Well, glad you're in the spirit."

He punched numbers into a machine and took Schew's handprint. Then put everything into a large black bag.

Schew turned and was about to take his things out to the van, when he saw it. The balding man said it was a nativity set. It was stunning. And almost life size. The man pointed out a Joseph and Mary, two shepherds, five sheep, three wise men, three camels and a baby Jesus in the manger. And that they were all lit from inside.

"I want those too," he said.

The man raised his eyebrows. "Are you sure? They're a complete set, so they're expensive. They're eighty years old."

"Yes, they're just what I've been looking for!" said Schew. He looked at the price tag. 4,899.00 Unity Credits. Well, he could take it out of savings. They must have that much in savings. He'd never find such a perfect set again.

In the end, all six of them were crammed in the van, along with their black bags of presents and the nativity set, with camels, sheep and wise men sticking out the windows. Joseph and Mary had to be tied to the roof of the van. The store owner had to put the manger in last and slam the door shut. It was nice of Eddie, who the bald man turned out to be, to help load. Especially since they had spent 7,486.00 Unity Credits at his store.

When the autovan got to the end of their block, they looked in amazement as their house glowed.

"Look at all the lights," said Four.

"I can't see," said Two.

"Brill," said Six.

"Wow," said Nine.

Mabel was silent, her face beamed with pleasure.

"See, now isn't this fun?" said Schew.

They deposited the nativity set onto the front lawn, then the podlings dropped their gifts in their own rooms. Schew hid his under the couch. He didn't know where Mabel put hers.

They decided to set up the nativity set in the back yard, by the swimming pool and the palm trees. The soft glow of the lights reflected off the green, murky pool, making it look like what Schew imagined a fairyland looked like. Although, he knew humans speculated as to whether fairies existed. But he'd seen a few, so he knew.

"What is the nativity set for?" asked Two.

"No idea," said Schew.

"It's some sort of story," said Six. "Something about Christmas."

"So, what are we going to do tomorrow?" asked Nine.

Mabel's feelers twitched in surprise.

"I think tomorrow we wrap gifts and put them by the tree," said Schew.

"Wrap them in what?" asked Mabel.

"I think we need to buy wrapping paper. And bows," he said.

"I like bows," said Four.

The next afternoon, they went shopping for gift wrap. It took five stores before they found the old fashioned stuff. Schew didn't want to buy the recyclable printed boxes and bags everyone was selling. How would he fit things like a guitar into a box? And given the sizes of bags the podlings had, he knew they'd have the same problem.

"How many tubes can we buy?" asked Six.

"I think we better buy quite a lot," said Mabel.

"We can always use what's leftover next year," said Schew. "I think ten tubes each."

They chose their favorites. And fifty bags of bows. And several packages of tissue paper. Then they carried their loot home and locked themselves in their rooms. Schew had to make a trip to the warehouse store to get a case of tape. They'd forgotten about that.

"Don't forget to mark on the outside of the present who it's for!" yelled Mabel from her work room.

It took all night. Mabel and Schew had to help Two and Four wrap their gifts. But by sunrise, they were finished.

They collected them in a corner of the living room.

The next evening, they brought the ladder in and stuck all the gifts onto the ceiling.

"Our house is so beautiful," sighed Two, looking up at the mixture of colored lights and presents crisscrossing the ceiling and in the middle, their Christmas tree.

"I think so too," whispered Mabel.

Schew thought so too.

"What are we doing tomorrow night?" asked Six.

"Well, what's left to do?" asked Schew.

"We need to plan Christmas dinner," said Mabel, "decide whether to go traditional or modern."

"Traditional," said Six.

"Modern," said Nine.

Two and Four shrugged. "Food," they said in unison.

"How about some of both?" asked Schew.

"Okay," Mabel said. "I'll plan a menu. Tomorrow, we shop. The next day we start cooking. We'll finish cooking on Christmas Day."

The next day on his lunch hour, Schew added up how much they'd spent. With horror, he realized they'd spent two entire paychecks. And more. And there was still food to buy. How did Earthlings do this? Every year! He felt uneasy about the amount of money they'd spent. He emptied the savings account. That should be enough to cover everything until he got paid again.

He flipped open the news on his screen. One of the local stories was about homeless shelters being full of people and short of money. He had to ask the elevator man before he could find anyone who knew what a homeless shelter was. Sam was the only human who worked in the building during the day. Everyone else was an Off Worlder. That was the polite phrase Earthlings called aliens.

"Homeless shelters are places for people to stay when they don't got no home," he said.

"What do you mean, no home?"

"'zactly that. No home, no house, no roof over they's head," said the elderly man. "They's broke and poor. No money."

"But why don't they have money? Why do they have no place to live?"

"No job. Or they's too sick, got kids to take care of, poisoned by alcohol or drugs. So many reasons."

Schew's mouth dropped open and his feelers stood on end. "And your world government doesn't take care of them?"

"Not good enough."

"That's awful. That is absolutely and totally wrong," he said. "And is this a big problem here on Earth?"

"Yessir. What you think all them bonfires about as you drive into town? People tryin' to stay warm. Livin' in the ruins of old buildings. It's horrible."

"My, my. I had no idea."

Schew was certain his Consulate Heads had no idea either. He immediately scheduled a meeting with them.

They filed into the meeting room, sitting on the hard metal chairs around a glass table, which enabled everyone to see what everyone else was doing with their feet and hands.

"No. We had no idea," said Fitch, his round face clouding with dark purple.

"Their government certainly has plenty of money," said Noga, his feelers twitching.

"We'll look into this," said Sanoj, waggling two of his legs back and forth. "This could mean sanctions."

"It'll take some time. We'll bring it up at the Unity meeting tomorrow, but Earth's Government moves at the speed of a slag-gaslug. And if they haven't taken care of this problem already, it means they don't want to. So they'll act even more slowly. This is not to be tolerated," said Fitch. "Thank you for bringing it to our attention. You deserve a promotion and a raise, young Setagean."

Schew went back to his office. He still felt terrible. Was there something he could do today?

After work, he, Mabel and the podlings shopped for food. They finally left the store with eight cartfuls of food. Schew didn't look at the total, just held his palm out to be scanned.

They spent the next two days cooking all manner of strange and familiar food. Then, they packed all the prepared food up in the van, along with all the gifts, piled themselves in where they could and drove to the homeless shelter. The shelter was packed with people looking for a meal.

It turned out that the shelter couldn't serve their food. They didn't have the right kind of permit. And the shelter had had a last minute donation of bright, shiny new gifts. They didn't want theirs. They wanted Unity credits.

Schew felt so disappointed. But he wasn't about to let his feelers droop in public. So, he got everyone back in the autovan and had it drive around.

"What are we looking for?" asked Nine.

"Bonfires and ruins," said Schew.

"Why?" asked Six.

"Because people live there who don't have money," he said.

It took an hour of driving before they found a bonfire. Nine people were huddled around it, even though the temperature was warm.

Schew got out and asked, "Do any of you want food or gifts?"

They stared at him.

He wondered if they could hear him. "Do any of you want food or gifts?" he yelled.

"Are you insulting us?" asked a woman.

"No, no insult meant. My family and I have too much food and too many gifts. This is our first Christmas and we just wanted to do things right. We'd like to share them."

"Well then," said a man, putting down a baseball bat. "Yes, we'd like to share."

Schew opened the back end of the van and they removed all the gifts. Then he and Mabel lay all the bowls and plates of various food out in the empty space.

"I forgot plates," said Mabel, her horrified eyes growing round with orange tinges around the edges.

"I've got plates and forks," said a man. "I collect 'em."

He hobbled over to a brick building which had a decided lean to it. It would probably fall down with the next quake. Another man followed him.

They returned with a box of fancy plates and silverware. And a cloth to dust them all off.

"Real china," he said proudly. "I'm Max."

"I've never seen such beautiful plates," said Mabel, running her fingers over one of them.

Schew watched as people dished up their food. Especially popular was the quilsa swon, a dish he and Mabel had as podlings. It was his favorite too.

"I never had food like this," cackled an old woman named Heather.

"It's a specialty from our planet," said Mabel.

They all sat around on boxes, or old chairs, eating, laughing and drinking from a bottle that was being passed around. Schew didn't know what was in it, but it made rubbing alcohol taste mild.

After eating, Two passed gifts around. She read the name of who it was intended for and closed her eyes, guessing who would like it.

"I've been looking for one of these for so long," said a middle aged man who got the bicycle tire pump. His name was John. "My bike tire's as flat as a pancake."

Louis got a tambourine from Four and began to play it. The guitar for Nine went to a June, who actually knew how to play it. Mabel got the scarf that Schew had gotten for her. It matched her feelers. Every single person got several gifts. The humans had each made or gotten gifts for each other and gave theirs away to the podlings, Mabel and Schew. Anybody who didn't like their gift, traded it to others for something they did want. In the end, everyone seemed happy.

Schew ended up with a little white ball and something called a golf club to hit the ball with. He decided to take it home and see how many times he could get it into the pool.

After they finished, they burned all the wrapping paper, except for one of the old women, Maris, who really liked hers and wanted to keep it. The fire roared into life.

June played her new guitar and sang 'Silent Night.' All the humans joined in. Schew had never heard anything quite so lovely. Then they sang a song called 'Jingle Bells' and taught his family the tune.

Finally, the celebration ended just as the sun was coming up.

One of the humans said, "I got to get to sleep."

The food was divided up between everyone. Gifts were loaded into the van. Everyone hugged and agreed to do the same thing next year, to meet here even if everyone had a new home. Schew really hoped Earth's government would do the right thing and take care of their people.

"That was the best Christmas ever," said one of the older men, Sam.

"That was the best Christmas possible," said Schew. He realized that all the money spent had been absolutely worth this moment and this feeling of unity.

"Next year will be even better," said Four.

"Just wait, I've got plans," said Two.

"The things we can do," said Six.

"It's the way Christmas should be," said Nine.

Schew couldn't think of anything else to add.

He just beamed.

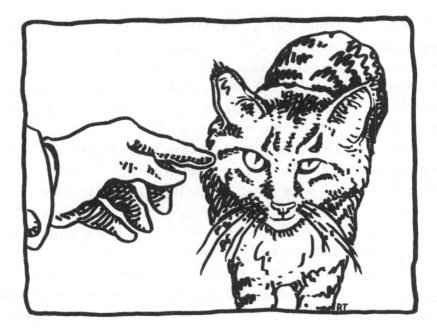

Marta and the Christmas Cat

Marta glanced at the clock on the wall. Her daughter, Sarah, would be here any time.

She went to the automatic checkout stand and hefted the bag of books and DVDs onto it. Then swiped her library card and checked out the four mystery novels and five movies, sliding each one back into the sturdy plastic bag decorated with sunflowers.

She went out into the entryway and buttoned up her coat then slipped on her knitted hat and gloves. The sun was out, but the day felt cold and crisp. Fresh snow blanketed everything.

Tomorrow it would probably turn to slush and mud, but today was bright and clean. She carefully walked outside, taking care not to slip on the ice. A man stood smoking just past the door. She crinkled her nose at the smell and walked away from it. Near the drop-off area, she swept snow from the bench with her gloves. Then she sat down next to the bronze sculpture of an old man with a dog and reading child at his feet. The statues were all outlined with snow. The parking lot was nearly empty. People around here tended to stay home when it snowed.

She'd always loved it. It made her feel like a child again, although she was fast approaching that second childhood of old age. She couldn't drive anymore. Had given that, and her car, up after a near accident. She'd moved into a retirement village. It had been easier than taking care of a big house and garden. Now she had an apartment with one bedroom and a bathroom: plus a living, dining room and tiny kitchen combined into one open room. She also had a little plot of earth about six feet long and a few pots to garden in. That was enough. She was eighty two after all.

The cold in the air made her breath visible, but she couldn't smell anything. Not even moisture in the air. Her coat wasn't quite thick enough for snow, still it was the warmest one she owned.

She missed looking out onto her old garden from the house. It had always been beautiful in the snow. She missed her home, and George, of course. He'd been gone two years now.

Marta had friends at her new home, but no one close. People mostly kept to themselves, despite the efforts of the staff to bring people together. Most of those who went to the events weren't people who she liked. They were loud, overly-friendly and desperate.

Well, she was probably desperate too. And lonely, for a quiet type of companionship. She didn't know what to do about that. It just was.

Some children were playing across the way, trying to make a snowman. School was on winter break, so the kids could fully enjoy the snow. Marta's daughter, Sarah, had dropped her off at the library and taken Marta's granddaughter to a friend's house for a sleepover. Then Sarah would come back and collect her.

Marta heard a meow and looked down. A scraggly, drenched tabby cat stood near one of the bushes.

"Hello," she said.

The cat came closer, limping.

"Did you hurt yourself, Dear?"

The cat meowed at her again and came close enough to be petted as Marta held out her hand.

"You must be cold despite all that fur."

The cat jumped up on the bench, still favoring the right paw. As Marta kept petting it, the cat climbed onto her lap and settled down, bathing and purring loudly, but shivering. Her fur was filled with tiny icicles.

"You're very friendly. And soaked completely through."

The cat was shivering, she noticed.

"This is not right. You don't have a home, do you?"

The bright green eyes looked at her as the cat meowed again.

Sarah's car drove up and stopped.

"That's me, I'm afraid," said Marta, gently setting the cat on the bench and petting it. She couldn't be sure if the cat was a stray. But it was so friendly, it must belong to someone. All the strays she'd seen at her old house were shy around strangers and would run away when they saw her.

It would be wrong to take someone's pet. Although, the cat didn't weigh much. It was all wet fur.

She stood and picked up her bag.

"I hope you find your way back home."

She walked to the car, opened the door and got in. But before she could close the door, the cat had vaulted onto her lap.

"Well, I guess you don't have a home, huh?"

Sarah just laughed.

"Mom, are you taking that cat home with you?"

"I don't know. It does seem to want to go with me."

"Does it have a collar?"

Marta felt around its neck. No collar or any sign of having worn one.

"No."

"Well, let's take it by my vet. See if there's a chip."

"A chip?" asked Marta, closing the car door.

"They put microchips in cats and dogs these days, so if the animal gets found, someone can contact the owner."

"Some people are so clever. Although, I don't think I'd like a chip put in me."

"You can talk and tell people where you live, animals can't."

Marta fastened her seat belt. The cat was burrowed into her wool coat, still shivering.

"Turn the heat up a bit, will you?" asked Marta. "I think this poor thing is so cold. It's shivering."

Sarah turned it up.

"Does your apartment allow pets?"

"Yes, they do. There's a limit, I think, though. Maybe a cat would be nice." As the ice on the cat's fur melted, it soaked into Marta's coat.

"It might not be housebroken."

"Well, we'll see. It sure is friendly. And no creature should be living out in the cold without any shelter. The poor thing's soaked."

At the vet's office, Sarah ran in to check if they could see the cat. Then ran back out.

"They can see us. They've had a lot of snow cancellations."

Sarah took the cat from her, so Marta could get out of the car.

"Oh, it's drenched," said the receptionist. "Let me get a towel."

The woman came back with a white towel and wrapped it around the cat, then led them back to an exam room.

"This will help the poor dear dry out. Where did you find it?"

"At the library," said Marta.

The cat simply cuddled into the towel, purring loudly, eyes closed as if it wanted to drift off to sleep.

"It stopped shivering," said Sarah.

The receptionist took down more information and said, "Doctor Shaw will be in shortly."

She closed the door behind her.

Marta held the cat in its towel and sat down on a bench.

A few minutes later the doctor came in holding a clipboard and carrying a piece of equipment that looked sort of like a large remote control.

Marta stood and put the cat and towel on the table.

"Good morning," said Doctor Shaw, a red-haired, middle aged woman. "I hear you found a stray."

"Well, I'm not sure. It's awfully friendly, jumped right into the car with no invitation. But it's cold and wet and limping."

"And you said the cat was shivering when you found it?"

"Yes."

The doctor petted the cat and held the towel back a bit so she could see the shoulders. Then she pointed the remote control thing at the cat's back and said, "No microchip."

Marta relaxed a bit and realized how much she wanted to take this cat home. She'd spent her life being responsible for everything and everyone. Then after George died, she'd fled from all responsibility and been miserable. She missed taking care of someone.

The doctor continued the exam, toweling the cat off and taking its temperature.

"The temperature's really low. If you keep it," the doctor rolled the cat on its back and examined its belly, "her … if you keep her warm and dry, she should be all right. She has fleas and a gash on her leg. I can dress that. Her eyes and ears look fine. If she's been living rough, which it looks like she has, she probably has worms. Someone owned her once, she's been spayed, at least."

The doctor got a new, dry towel and wrapped the cat up again. She checked her mouth and said, "She's an older girl, maybe ten, eleven years old.

"I'll get the right bandage and clean out her wound. I'm assuming you'd like to treat her for fleas and worms."

"Yes," said Marta. "What about shots?"

"We could do that today. It would be good to get her protected."

"Good," said Marta.

The doctor left the room.

Marta smiled.

She petted the cat who hadn't stopped purring yet.

"You're coming home with me honey. I hope that's what you wanted."

The doctor shaved some hair around the cut, cleaned and bandaged the wound.

"It's not bad, she must have cut it on a nail or something, but I don't want her licking it."

Then the cat was given a worm pill, flea medicine and shots.

"Good girl," said Marta, petting her.

"She's big and has quite a lot of hair. Might have some Maine Coon blood in her," said the vet. "You should brush her if she'll let you. That'll avoid a lot of hairballs."

"Mom, you're going to need to get some supplies," said Sarah.

"You're right, I am."

"We've got a few things out front," said the doctor.

In no time they bought a brush, with a razor in it, to thin the cat's hair a bit, grain free food, two bowls, cat litter made from wood pellets and a litter box, plus a couple of cat toys. All for an enormous amount of money, but it was convenient. The receptionist threw in a cardboard cat carrier and a dry towel to keep the cat warm on the ride home.

Sarah put all the purchases in the cat carrier, because Marta wasn't going to let the cat go for the ride home.

"She needs to be warm," was the defense Marta used. "I'll use the cat carrier next time."

The drive home was fast. Marta only lived five minutes from the vet. It was a small town, after all.

Sarah carried the library bag and cat supplies inside, and Marta brought the cat. Her apartment entrance shared a long interior hallway with other apartments.

Once inside Marta's rooms, Sarah set up the litter box in the bathroom and put the cat in it. She obviously understood and did her business.

Marta washed the bowls and filled one with water and the other with a bit of wet food. The cat who'd been exploring the apartment came running at the sound of the can opener. She still limped, but not as badly.

"Well, she *has* lived with someone," said Sarah.

The cat ate as if she hadn't in a very long time.

"I hope she doesn't bother your Christmas tree."

"It's fake, so hopefully it won't attract her. The decorations aren't breakable." She turned the Christmas lights and tree on. Then turned on the TV with the station that played Christmas music.

"What are you going to name her?"

"I don't know. I guess I'll need to live with her a while. Find out who she is."

"Well, I better get going," said Sarah. "I've got to figure out dinner and cook before Jim gets home."

"Thank you for the ride and all the help," said Marta, hugging her daughter.

"Glad I could be of help. I'll call you on Sunday, when Jim's ready to come pick you up."

"That will be perfect."

She was going to their house for Christmas.

Marta opened a can of soup for lunch and sat and ate, watching the cat bathe herself by the glass door which led to her fenced garden and patio. Her patio table and chairs were coated with a couple of inches of snow. An ornamental grass and a dwarf pine made peculiar white shapes.

Snow made the world look so different.

After lunch Marta sat on the couch. She folded up an afghan beside her and patted it. The cat jumped up on it purring and Marta petted her soft fur, which had finally dried. The cat was amazingly fluffy.

"I think you and I will get along just fine."

The cat curled up and slept while Marta listened to Christmas music and crocheted.

This was going to be the most lovely Christmas she'd had in some time.

Merry. She'd name the cat Merry. Because that's how the cat made her feel.

"Merry. How do you like that name."

"Mrow," the cat chirruped drowsily, purring louder.

Both their hearts filled with warmth.

We Wish You a Merry Christmas

Milena Alexander didn't know how she was going to deal with Christmas again. She sat in the bustling coffee shop at a tiny table by herself, sipping a skinny latte with rice milk sprinkled with cinnamon and nutmeg. She'd added too much cinnamon. It almost made her sneeze.

The woman at the next table had two squirming children, one young enough to have a diaper top poking out the top of her pants. The other not much older. The woman was texting on her phone oblivious to her two kids arguing over a teddy bear and sipping their drinks; hot chocolate from the look of the rings around their mouths.

The sound system blared the latest version of 'We Wish You a Merry Christmas', sung by some pop star whose voice was familiar, but she couldn't put a name or face to. Milena was tired of hearing Christmas music. It had been nearly a month since work had started playing them. Every single day, every single minute. She could hardly wait till January.

The coffee shop was filled with people carrying huge bags of Christmas presents. All the nearby stores were having sales. Milena had thought that coming here might cheer her up, get her into the spirit of things. All she could do was look at everyone who had money to buy gifts and be content with her splurge of a latte. Christmas was miserable when there was no one to share it with. She didn't even have enough money to buy herself out of a funk.

Christmas used to be magical for her. When had that ended? Why had she lost that?

She didn't have to think hard about that. She'd lost the magic when Mom and Dad died on Christmas Eve. Her Christmases had been miserable ever since.

It was only four weeks away. She wanted to run away on a vacation to somewhere Christmas wasn't celebrated. For maybe like, forever.

She'd moved out to Seattle to go to college, hoping to get hired afterwards at a tech company and be able to pay her student loans off quickly. It'd been a good plan. But she wasn't a good enough programmer or technical writer to make the cut. Anywhere.

So she ended up staying with her college job, working at a large store selling clothes that she couldn't really afford to wear. But she bought them anyway, because the job called for it.

Milena finished her coffee without really tasting it and left the coffee shop. She walked beneath the covered walkways out of the pouring rain. It was her day off and yet, she found herself in the same area where she worked. Better than sitting at home doing laundry or cleaning her tiny spartan apartment once again.

It sucked to be broke and alone at Christmas. At least she didn't have anyone she had to buy gifts for. All her formerly close friends from college had gotten jobs in California and moved down there. Now that they were working eighty hours a week, they had no time for friendships.

The wind picked up and she zipped her coat up higher around her neck, fluffing up the scarf over it. Her boots rose up over her leggings, keeping her feet dry and warm, but she needed a hat. A month ago, on a whim she'd whacked off all her hair, cutting it about an inch short all over. Then realized that perhaps she should have done that during summer. It looked cute, but wasn't exactly practical. She'd see if she could find a hat on the discount table at work.

She walked for about three hours, around and around the shopping complex, watching the grumpy couple shopping, the woman on a mission to finish all her shopping in one trip, the newly in love couple laughing at everything.

She met those people every day at work. She loved watching little kids go through the stores. Their eyes popping out of their heads at all the glitz and shiny.

Seeing the kids just made her more depressed. She'd grown to hate this time of year and working retail made it even worse.

Mom and Dad had died in the car accident on Christmas Eve two years ago coming back from church. Dad's night vision was probably bad and the snow was awful in Montana that winter. The car had slipped on black ice and rammed straight into a five foot pile of snow which hid a telephone pole.

She'd flown home after the police called her. Spent all of Christmas Day in airports trying to get to Missoula. It was hell, seeing everyone happy when her heart felt ripped to shreds. Why hadn't she gone home that break? Too worried about how she'd done on her finals and whether she'd make it through the year. Plus the chance to make lots of money working overtime during the break.

The doctors tried to save them, but in the end nothing worked. And Milena spent her Christmas break trying to sell all their stuff, arrange funerals and pay huge hospital bills with the sales. In the end, what was left over didn't even pay for her plane ticket. And she was left an orphan. A twenty year old orphan, but an orphan all the same.

She went back to school that January numb and exhausted. Two years later, she still hadn't recovered. And she now hated Christmas, had no close friends and a job that paid her basic bills and after that, there was nothing left. No frills, no potential car or house. Certainly not the American Dream. If everything went well, she'd be done paying back her student loans in ten years. She'd be thirty-two years old!

So, a mere ten more years of living like this to look forward to. No going out to eat. No pay raises, since she was pretty much at the top of the pay scale. Of course, everything else would go up, food, medical, rent, student loans, etc.

Walking around the shopping center was not helping her feel happier. She should have just stayed home.

Milena set off across the parking lot and down towards the Cut. Maybe a walk over by the water would help. Away from people so she wouldn't feel so alone.

The rain had stopped, but the tall bare trees dripped big splats down on her face. It was always so gray here, maybe she should try again to get hired down in California. Or maybe try the tech companies around here again. But she was a year behind everything now. She hadn't even tried to keep up on new advances in the tech world.

The air grew colder as she came to the water. She found a dirt path and followed it, beneath the bridge, watching the mallards swim in the water. Putting their heads down for food. What did they find to eat here? Surely there weren't any fish. A couple of boats came down the Cut from the west from Lake Union or the Sound. More people with money.

Finally, she came to a bench and sat down, tucking her long coat beneath her. She was already about as wet as she could get. A wet bench wouldn't matter much.

A couple dressed in heavy duty rain gear came past her, each carrying a kayak and paddle. She just shook her head. Seattleites were crazy.

They put the kayaks in the water and got in, then paddled off towards Lake Washington.

The grayness around her lightened slightly, as if the sun was making an attempt to burn through the clouds. People walked, rode and rolled past on the concrete trail nearby.

A frail old woman with long gray braids, dressed in a yellow raincoat and wearing black rubber boots slowly sat down on the bench at the other end. She leaned a carved wooden cane up against the bench. Her wrinkled face looked tan for this being winter, but not trip to Hawaii or tanning bed tan. It looked like she spent a lot of time outside.

She slowly took a bag off her shoulder, smiled at Milena and pulled yarn out of the bag and began to crochet, her hands quickly moving yarn and hook. She wore fingerless gloves and her fingers flashed stitch after stitch. It was hypnotizing how fast she crocheted. Unreal.

Milena watched her without trying to be obvious. She hadn't seen anyone crochet since Nanna had stopped. Her eyesight got bad pretty quickly before the end. Milena had been what, fifteen when she died?

The old woman knotted green, red and silver yarn together into little squares. Milena had seen Nanna make those. Then she had hooked all the square together into a throw and given it to Milena.

Wouldn't that be fun to try? And she liked the colors.

The woman glanced up and caught her watching, smiled at Milena.

"I'm making a blanket for my sister. I think she needs a little Christmas cheer this year. She just lost her daughter," she said, patting her work.

"Oh, I'm sorry," said Milena. "It looks beautiful."

"Thank you. You don't look too cheery yourself. I'm sorry, I always saying things I shouldn't."

"No, you're right. I don't feel very Christmassy."

"Well, that happens. I suppose you've tried all the things they recommend, volunteering your time to help others, getting enough rest, taking your vitamin D."

"Yeah. I volunteer at the food bank once a week, get eight hours of sleep and take my vitamins, especially D. Nothing seems to help."

"Broke?"

"Yep."

"Alone?"

"Yep."

"Well, that sucks," said the old woman. "I'm Maggie."

"Milena."

"I don't mean to be forward, but I'm having a little get together tonight at my place. Just a few friends. We bring whatever we're working on, crochet, knitting, embroidery, drawing and sit around and chat about whatever comes up. I just baked cookies and there'll be hot spiced cider. It's very informal. You're welcome to come. 7:00."

"I'm not working on anything. I don't know how to do anything." Milena's first instinct was to pull away. It's what she always did. It's why she didn't have any friends right now. She should say yes and go, she knew. "I'm not creative."

"Sure you are. You're human. To be human is to be creative. You just need to practice something, anything. Come tonight and I'll teach you something. I've got scads of yarn."

"Okay," she said.

"Well, I'd better get going on home," said Maggie, stuffing her crocheting back in the bag. "I need to tidy up before people come." She gave Milena a card with her name and address on it.

Milena watched the old woman pick up her cane and walk towards the parking lot, getting into a cab which had been parked there, waiting.

Milena looked at the address the woman had given her. It was only a few blocks from where she lived.

She was afraid she'd chicken out at the last minute.

'What are you afraid of?' she asked herself on the walk back to her apartment. She knew what it was. First, she was afraid of getting hurt. But deeper than that, she felt afraid of having fun. She didn't deserve it. And that was total crap. But it sat there, hunkered down deep within, that black belief, taking up far too much space.

She'd gotten rid of it before. Banished, but the feeling always came back. And she felt weary of it, tired of trying to make it go away and tired of the negativity.

So, she went.

At 7:00PM she stood before Maggie's little cottage just north of the University District.

Maggie answered the door. Milena walked into the cozy living room filled with overstuffed chairs, bookshelves and a gas stove masquerading as a wood stove. The walls were covered with bookshelves or paintings in various styles or tapestries. The small kitchen opened up at the other end and a table laden with desserts, plates and mugs, surrounded by six chairs, sat in between the two rooms. The house was stuffed with interesting things to look at and Milena would have loved to live here. It felt warm and loving, not like her bare, cold apartment.

Which pretty much summed up her life right now.

Two women were there already sitting near the gas stove, one knitting and the other quilting.

"This is Heather, and Sheila," Maggie said. "And this is Milena."

"Hi," said Sheila, a dowdy, gray haired woman looked up from her quilting.

"Glad you could come," said Heather, who had long auburn hair, which didn't look like it was her own color. Heather looked closer to her own age, maybe just a little older.

"I'm glad I could make it," said Milena. "Thanks for inviting me."

"Well, we're still waiting for Poppy and Judith to arrive, but they're usually late. So, here's all my extra yarn," Maggie said, pointing to a large round table piled high with old plastic milk crates full of yarn. It looked like a rainbow, there were so many colors. "I've got all sorts of patterns and all sizes of crochet hooks. Why don't you take a look at this book, all the patterns are fairly easy. Find something that looks interesting to make. I'll start pouring the spiced cider."

Milena took the book and sat in one of the chairs. It looked poofy, like one of those chairs which ate you, but it felt firm and easy to sit on. She flipped through the book which had patterns for placemats, dish towels, purses and bags, and throws. Milena had already decided she wanted to make a throw.

Nana, now long gone, had made a throw for her. Red and green. She'd loved it until it fell to bits. She'd make a Christmassy throw, even though she probably wouldn't finish it in the next three weeks.

When Maggie brought her a cup of hot cider, Milena pointed to a pattern and said, "How about this one."

"Oh, that's lovely. I think that's a great place to start. So you'll need three different colors of yarn. Why don't you choose colors you'd like to use?"

Maggie went back for more mugs while Milena looked at the yarns. It was sort of overwhelming to choose from the huge selection.

She finally narrowed it down to a rich deep green, a warm red and a crisp white. All of the yarns were very soft and fuzzy and felt good to her skin. But there wasn't very much of them. Surely not enough to make a good sized throw.

"Oh, those will be beautiful," said Maggie.

"But there's not enough yarn, is there?"

"No, but I got them from Judith. She spun and dyed them. We'll see if she has more of those colors."

There was a knock on the door and Maggie went to answer it. "Speak of the devil."

Two women came in, one tall and elegant looking with shoulder length dark hair and wearing a black A-line skirt with a classic white blouse and pumps. The other short, frumpy and dressed in a dazzling number of colors which would have shocked the fashion nazis at work. It was as if the clothes she wore were meant to ward off the gray, rainy days of December. Just looking at her made Milena smile.

Maggie took their wet coats and hung them on hooks next to a radiator, where all the other coats hung.

"Judith, Poppy, this is Milena. Milena this is Poppy and this tall drink of water is Judith, the one who spins and dyes yarn."

"Hi," said Milena.

"Good evening," said Judith.

"Merry whatever it is you celebrate," said Poppy.

"Judith, Milena is starting her first crocheting project and she chose your yarns to do it, but I don't have enough of the colors she wants to use. Do you have any left at home, from the same dye lot?"

Judith put down her bags by a chair and came over and looked at the yarns, "Lucifer red, yes, Angel's wing white, yes. And what green is this," she asked, turning the bundle over to read the tag. "Summer grass green, I think I have that one, yes. I can bring more next week," she said. "Since it's your first project, I'll give them to you for free. Merry Christmas, or Happy Hanukkah, or Peaceful Solstice, or whatever."

"Are you sure?" asked Milena. "Hand spun yarn must be expensive."

"Normally, yes. But I've had a good year. I sell it online and shows and I can afford to give things away. It's good karma."

"Thank you," said Milena, she felt grateful to be included by complete strangers.

Maggie sat down next to her and showed her how to do the main stitches. Then let Milena go to it, until she finished with one color. Then she showed her how to attach the next color and Milena carried on.

Poppy was working on crocheting and beading fancy flowers which she attached to the prettiest felted bags. Maggie continued working on her throw and Judith spun yarn from clumps of cream colored wool.

"Tomorrow I get to dye," she said. "It's the most fun. I'm always surprised by what colors take to the wool more intensely. It's like opening Christmas gifts."

Milena felt useful for the first time in so long. She was actually making something tangible. And it was easy! It looked pretty and felt so soft.

They stopped about halfway through the evening and ate buttery Christmas cookies and drank more cider. Maggie, Poppy and Sheila seemed to have known each other for a long time, they met at a knitting class years ago and Maggie had decided to form Maggie's Monday Night Sewing Circle.

"My mother used to go to one when I was little," she said. "I decided I needed something like that in my life, a community of women who got together to create things. One night Sheila brought Heather and she stayed. And one night Poppy brought Judith and she was hooked too. Sometimes people stay and sometimes not. It depends on what they need in their lives at the moment."

"Well, I'd like to stay," said Milena.

"I thought you might," said Maggie. "You're really making good progress."

"I never thought it would be so much fun." Milena said.

After eating they went back to the living room and chattered on while they worked. Milena mostly listened to them talk about politics, movies, books and music. When was the last time she had conversations like this with friends? Her coworkers didn't talk about anything except clothes and their lovers.

By the end of the night she'd finished a good sized strip of the throw. Several more evenings like this and she could see it being finished. The thought shocked her. She hadn't actually made things since she was a little girl. A clay pot, long gone, in elementary school. A painting class had led to several canvases in middle school, also tossed in the garbage years ago. None of them had turned out well.

Judith had finished spinning all her wool. Sheila had a few more squares on her quilt done. Heather's sweater was beginning to take shape. Maggie had finished many more rows on her throw and Poppy had attached all the beaded, crocheted flowers onto her felt bags.

"Those are so beautiful," Milena told Poppy.

"Thank you, which one do you like the best?" she asked.

They were all beautiful, but Milena pointed to a warm khaki colored bag with cream, blush pink and salmon colored flowers.

"That one, I think. The colors are so subtle, but so perfect."

"It's yours," said Poppy. "You'll need something to carry your yarn and throw home in."

"I couldn't," said Milena.

"Yes, you could and you must," said Poppy.

"But I have nothing to give you. I could give you this throw when it's done." Although she didn't really want to. She felt a need to give Poppy something. Those bags would probably sell for a couple hundred dollars online.

"No, you don't need to give me anything. You should always keep the first thing you make for yourself to remind yourself never to stop making things. When we stop creating, it's the beginning of a slow death," said Poppy, holding the bag out to Milena.

"Thank you, it's just perfect," she said, taking the soft bag. What an incredible gift.

She put her skeins of yarn in the beautiful bag, along with the part of the throw that she'd finished and the crochet hook.

"See you all same time next week," said Maggie.

"We'll be here," the others said.

"Me too," said Milena.

The next week flew by in a flash. The brutal weeks before Christmas, someone always got sick and everyone else ended up working overtime. Milena hurried home every night and worked on her throw while watching movies. The throw grew and grew. She poured all her energy into it. Memories of Christmases spent with Mom and Dad rose to the surface, were cried about and lingered. By the time Maggie's Monday Night Sewing Circle rolled around, Milena felt limp with exhaustion and she'd run out of yarn.

She worked Monday until six, grabbed a bus home and a couple of cheese sticks and her bag with the throw and crochet hook in it and ran out the door to Maggie's. She was so tired and burned out from dealing with customers who wanted everything,

Of course, three weeks before Christmas, the store probably didn't have what they wanted. It had plenty of clothes, but never the right size or color. That was a little known rule about Christmas.

One of the other ones was that Christmas comes at the same time every year. So people shouldn't wait until the weeks before Christmas to shop.

Another was to be nice to the poor retail folks who were there to help you.

She showed up at Maggie's only a few minutes late and out of breath. It was dry tonight, so she wasn't soaking wet. Inside the stove poured out heat and everyone looked cheery and was working away.

"Sorry I'm late. Had to work overtime today," Milena said, taking her coat off.

"Well, that'll be good for your pocketbook," said Judith.

"But not so good for the soul, come on in, take a load off. Tonight I made Wassail. It's got brandy in it, if you'd like some. It does pack a punch," said Maggie.

"I'd love some," said Milena. "I've never had it."

"Apple cider, brandy, spices, it's wonderful," said Heather.

Maggie handed Milena a mug of the warm beverage. She sipped it and it felt as if she woke up for the first time today.

"Well, welcome to the real world," said Sheila.

Milena laughed.

"I brought more yarn for you," said Judith. She put three more skeins of each color out on the bare coffee table for Milena.

"Oh, thank you. I ran out last night."

"Well, you have been busy," said Maggie.

"I have. I've worked on it every night this week, watching movies after work. Because working retail at Christmas doesn't leave me with much of a brain."

"I used to do that," said Poppy. "It was fun, but deadening."

"What do you do now?" asked Milena, as she began crocheting on the throw.

"I make a living off selling my bags," she said. "It's so much more fun. I'm my own boss and I get to introduce new products to my store when I get bored. I get to use the colors I like and basically, do what I want."

"Tell me Poppy, what colors don't you like?" asked Judith, smiling.

"Okay, okay, I like them all, but I get to combine them in whatever way I want."

They all laughed. Poppy was again dressed like a rainbow. She simply glowed. As a matter of fact, they all did, but she was the most obvious.

As they talked Milena's fingers sped along effortlessly making row after row of stitches. Each one looked almost perfect. And she didn't even have to think about it. Her thoughts wandered.

Sheila was selling her quilts. Judith was selling her yarn. Heather was selling her sweaters. They were all making a living off what they loved to do.

"Maggie do you sell your throws?" asked Milena.

"Me, no. I'm a retired professor from the U. I've always lived simply and saved money. So I just make my throws for friends and neighbors. Sometimes I donate them to a hospice. I also make baby blankets for the hospital. They give them to newborns. I'm lucky enough that I don't have to actually work anymore."

Milena nodded and started a new row with the green yarn. Was there something she could be good enough at, that there was a market for, that she could sell? Wouldn't it be wonderful to quit her job? Or maybe not even quit, just pay off her student loans. Have enough money left over to go out to eat.

It seemed that in Maggie's house, Milena could crochet faster and easier than normal. Or perhaps it was the company. But her stitches became more even and seemed to fly off the crochet hook as she listened to the conversation. By the time she was ready to leave a third of the throw was finished.

Sheila looked up from her quilting and said, "Maggie, you look tired tonight. Have you been overdoing it?"

"Of course I have," said Maggie. "Time is short when you get as old as I am. And there's so much left to do. So much life left to live."

Milena wondered just how old Maggie was.

The next Monday, Milena was worn out from working six days in a row and more overtime nearly every day. She plunked down in a chair. The aroma of chocolate and cinnamon filled the air. Heat from the stove warmed her and the soft lighting and quiet voices made her feel calm and revived.

She'd finished the throw and brought it for people to see. It wasn't perfect, but she felt proud of it.

"Oh, that's lovely," said Maggie, looking at her throw. She hadn't gotten up from her chair. Sheila served them the Mexican Hot Chocolate.

"Beautiful," said Judith. "What are you going to make next?"

"I found a pattern for a sort of shawl crossed with a scarf, I think that's what I want to make," she said, turning to the page in the book to show them.

"Ooh, I love that," said Poppy. "What color?"

Milena pulled the rose colored yarn she'd bought earlier in the week out of her bag.

"I've got a gray wool dress that I love, but it needs something like this to brighten it up."

"That should be beautiful together," said Sheila.

By the end of the night, Milena had learned all the stitches she'd need and gotten quite a ways into the scarf. Everyone had shared their events from the last week, except Maggie.

Finally, she said, "I've got some news. And it's not good, but it is what it is."

"What?" asked Poppy, wrinkles forming on her forehead.

"You know I haven't been feeling my usual self. It's as I thought, my cancer's back. This time it's spreading very, very quickly. The doctors have said there's not much they can do besides keep me comfortable."

She could see Poppy chewing on her lip, biting back tears. Sheila's hands began shaking.

Milena's mouth dropped open and her heart sank.

Poppy got up and bent over to hug Maggie, who patted Poppy's arm.

Judith said, "How is that possible?

Heather said, "Oh no!"

Milena felt the vast empty blackness inside her well up and threaten to smother her again. She'd just found a circle of friends and now it would all end. She'd be alone again. And it was two weeks until Christmas.

She shook herself. How incredibly selfish. 'Maggie's just told us she's dying and you're worried about yourself.'

"What can I do to help?" asked Milena.

"Oh honey, I'm really not sure yet. I will need help since I'll be moving into the hospice this week."

"Call me when you know what you need," said Milena.

"I'm available to help," said Sheila.

"Me too," said Heather.

Judith and Poppy nodded their heads.

"I'll organize us volunteers," said Judith. "Maggie you tell me what you need when and I'll find one of us to get it done. I don't want you to spend all your energy trying to hunt each of us down every time you need something."

"Thank you," said Maggie. "I can't tell you how much this means to me."

"Did the doctors tell you how long?"

"Probably less than a couple of weeks," said Maggie. "And the pain killers are making me far too groggy. There's so much I still want to do.

"Do you still want to keep hosting us?" asked Poppy.

"Yes, up until I can't anymore," she said.

Milena went home and tried not to sink into a deep depression. She hurt just thinking about Maggie. But at least she could help. She wrote out a list of things that she could do to make Maggie's last weeks on Earth an easier place to be.

She worked on the shawl and finished it rather quickly. It looked perfect with her gray dress. Then she set to work secretly making a colorful throw for Maggie.

She helped Maggie gather the things she wanted to take with her to the hospice and organized her clothes and other belongings to give to Maggie's friends or donate them to charity.

Milena cheerfully spent both of her days off at Maggie's. The house needed cleaning, there was laundry to do and meals to make. Although, Maggie wasn't eating much.

"What are you going to do with all your furniture and books?" asked Milena.

"They'll stay with the house. I think the new owner might like some of them."

"So, you've sold the house already."

"Not yet," said Maggie, arching an eyebrow playfully.

Milena didn't know what that meant.

The next meeting of Maggie's Monday Night Sewing Circle happened at the hospice. It was a week before Christmas. Poppy brought hot chocolate and Heather brought a chocolate coffee-cake.

They sat around and chatted. Maggie's hands were too shaky to crochet and she looked very weak, but she seemed to enjoy the company. Milena gave Maggie the soft light blue and green throw she'd made.

"Oh, this is wonderful and so soft. Thank you. I don't have many pleasures left, but touch is definitely one of them."

Milena worked on a purple cap. Heather was finishing another sweater to sell, Sheila another quilt, Poppy decorated more felted bags and Judith knitted beautiful striped socks. Maggie watched them all, beaming at their progress.

"I'm so glad you all came," she said.

"We're going to miss you so much," said Sheila.

They all nodded.

"You are going to keep meeting, aren't you?" asked Maggie.

"We haven't talked about it," said Judith.

"I think you should," said Maggie.

"I'm not sure that meeting without you, or someplace other than your home would be anything like the same," said Poppy, wiping a tear from her face.

"Of course it won't be the same," said Maggie, "but it will still be wonderful. And who knows, the new person who lives in my house might like having a sewing circle there."

"Who is moving into your house?" asked Heather.

"It's a surprise," said Maggie. "You'll just have to be patient and find out."

Maggie died later that night, a smile on her face the nurses said. Milena wept for days. She took the day off work to go to the funeral. The sewing circle were all there and a few of Maggie's relatives, her sister and brother, both a year younger than Maggie, neither of them in great health.

Milena felt a void in her life. Somehow, she made it through work the next few days, but barely. She was making a pair of fingerless gloves, still not sure what might sell best online. She needed to make whatever it was, her own style. Make it original somehow. That part hadn't come to her yet.

Later in the week, Milena got a letter from a lawyer asking her to be present at the reading of Maggie's will. She traded days off with a coworker and went, wearing her gray dress and rose colored shawl.

The only people present were the sewing circle. Apparently, Maggie hadn't left anything to her brother or sister, the lawyer quoted a letter he'd sent to them. 'You've both told me a hundred times that you have too much junk, and of course so do I, so I know you don't want mine. I don't have a lot of money left, not after paying all these medical bills and I know you and your families aren't hurting for money, so I'll give my pittance away to people who are hurting for money. I love both of you very much and I'll see you again when you get here. Wherever here is."

The lawyer read Maggie's will, which gave each of the sewing circle various keepsakes of Maggie's. Sheila got her teapot, she'd always admired. Heather a wall hanging. Judith an antique spindle and Poppy, a painting. Milena got Maggie's entire collection of yarn, crochet books and hooks, which were still at Maggie's house.

They each left, saying they'd meet the Monday after next at Poppy's house, and not just because Maggie had said she wanted them to keep meeting. Everyone missed the circle.

Milena arranged to meet the lawyer the following day to pick up the yarn and books. Poppy volunteered to drive her, because Milena wasn't sure she could carry everything in one trip.

The lawyer was already there when they arrived that afternoon. He handed Milena an envelope and said, "You'd better read this first."

Milena opened the envelope and pulled out a handwritten letter which read:

Dearest Milena,

I wanted to give you a helping hand, just as others have helped me along. I know you've had a rough few years, emotionally and financially, and I hope this rectifies things.

I'm giving you my house because I know you'll treat her well.

She's a magical little house and appreciates being loved. She's all paid for, you'll just owe taxes, insurance and utilities, so hopefully you'll come out better for not having to pay that astronomical rent! If you sell her, please make sure she goes to a loving owner.

I'm also giving you the money in my savings account. Hopefully, it'll pay off some of your student loans and you'll be closer to achieving whatever your dreams.

I encourage you to keep the Monday Night Sewing Circle going. It's given me years of pleasure and I'm thinking it might do the same for you.

Work hard and may you have good luck creating your dreams,

Love,

Maggie

Milena's mouth hung open. Maggie had given her the house! She could hardly believe it.

"What's it say?" asked Poppy.

Milena handed her the letter. Poppy read it and started jumping up and down.

"Good thing I brought the pickup. You ready to move?"

"No. I've packed nothing. I had no idea."

"That Maggie. She's sneaky that way," said Poppy, laughing. She got on the phone and in an hour, after Milena signed a lot of papers, the entire sewing circle was at Milena's apartment.

"Moving party," said Heather.

They filled up boxes and bins which they'd brought, wrapped Milena's thrift store dishes and packed away her clothes. Milena had never bought a lot of stuff. She always owed too much money. It took about two hours to pack everything and load it into the two cars, a van and a small pickup. By nightfall all her belongings were in Maggie's old house. Milena's new house. A lot of her furniture sat in Maggie's empty garage. Milena had a feeling that she'd be having a garage sale next summer.

110

The house was filled with her boxes and they could barely walk around. Pizza was delivered and everyone crammed into the kitchen to eat. Milena had turned the radio on, even though it played Christmas music, which she was tired of, she needed to listen to it, to help believe that this was all real.

"I expect you to have this all unpacked and put away by Monday," said Poppy.

"Yeah, we'll need to meet at your house now," said Judith.

Milena just smiled.

The radio began playing "We Wish You a Merry Christmas" and they all sang along.

Because it was, for the first time in a very long while.

It felt as if Maggie was still there with them.

Celena Davis-Dunivent
Lake Stevens, WA

She is crazy, sassy, and loves being an original. A recent high school graduate, nanny and writer. Her head is always full of new ideas and with her unique personality she strives to be creative in multiple forms. She has a passport and intends to fill it.

You can contact Celena through the Writers Cooperative of the Pacific Northwest website: writers-coop.com

Twenty Cookies and a Plane Ticket
Winter's Day
Fall

Twenty Cookies and a Plane Ticket

I woke up Christmas day of 2009, I was ten years old and didn't know this was going to be one of my lifelong, favorite memories. My grandma, Yaya, and I were dropped off at the airport early in the morning with our suitcases, a carry-on bag, and a gift box of packaged cookies. I gave the first small package to the man at the baggage drop. His face lit up with my simple act of gratitude, so I presented another at security and wished them a Merry Christmas.

We were all checked in and looked for our gate when we stopped at the restroom. An attendant was cleaning the sink. On my way out I tried to give her some cookies. At first, she refused to take it, but after a couple more tries, she accepted the package. Then she told me, with a heavy Russian accent, "You stay in school! You don't want to clean bathroom on Christmas." It made me joyous to give away all five packages of cookies, before boarding the plane. We were on our way to Illinois to visit my great-grandfather, who we all called Grandbob.

When we landed in Bloomington, we just made it out of the terminal, when Yaya and I were greeted by my Grandbob and his second wife, Joyce. After giving hugs, we walked to the baggage claim and then to Joyce's car, going straight to their house. We had another Christmas celebration with a gift exchange, followed by a small dinner. Finally, we each had a bowl of ice cream before bed.

The next day, after breakfast I got ready to go play in the snow. That is when I met the neighbor behind Grandbob's house. There was a girl about my age playing alone in the adjoining backyard. At first, we tentatively waved at each other and began talking and throwing snowballs over the fence. As the day went on, Violet and I played for a long time until it was nearly dark and we were both called in to dinner.

I helped set the dinner table and took the seat next to Grandbob. During our meal, he showed me a trick to make it appear that you are pulling your hair back and forth like it's a wig. As soon as the meal was done, and the mess cleaned, I baked cookies with Grandma Joyce and poured two glasses of milk. We sat by the fireplace with fresh cookies before we all went to bed.

The next day I woke up before everyone else, or I thought I did. I quietly snuck out of the bedroom and down the stairs where I was greeted by Grandma Joyce. "Good morning," she said to me as I walked into the room. She finished reading a page in a newspaper so we could work together and make breakfast.

We heard the booming voice of my Grandbob, "What's for breakfast girls?" followed by Yaya's greeting.

"Just smell; it's cinnamon rolls!" I said excitedly. "They are baking in the oven." We continued to scramble eggs and put together a bowl of mixed fruits and smoothies. Not the usual bowl of cereal I was used to.

After breakfast, I found stockings hanging on the fireplace. Once we were done, I ran to play outside building snowmen and making snow angels. I learned to ice skate on that trip with my new friend. One night I learned about mistletoe and watched the Three Stooges with Grandbob as dinner was being made. I sat on his lap in the recliner as he told stories, and we laughed until one of us peed. (I won't say who.)

I have beautiful memories of a hundred holidays, but that Christmas will be held close to my heart, and I look forward to sharing the story with my own children so they can learn about Grandbob, a one of a kind grandparent.

Winter's Day

Frost covers the windows
All the kiddies wake with joy
As the ground is covered in snow
They all hurry to go out and play
Each one to do it their own way
Making snow Angels
Building forts
Having snowball fights
Making snowmen
Sledding all day long
By the end of the day
The kiddies all go home
Where it's nice and warm
And drink hot chocolate
And sit by the fire with their families

Fall

The crisp air blows gently through the trees
Leaves crunch under our feet with every step
Colors of the trees change from green
Everyone drinking warm apple cider
Wearing sweaters and scarves
When they go outside to play
Some trees are bare, as the last leaf falls
Perfect for raking and jumping in the piles
Nights are longer as the days shorten
Perfect for watching fall movies
Knowing that, winter will be here soon

Sonya Rhen
Kirkland, WA

Sonya Rhen is the author of the humorous Space Tripping series. She lives on the "Eastside" with her husband, two children, two cats and a very anxious dog. When she's not writing you might find her dancing.
https://sonyarhen.wordpress.com/

Gift of the Stars
A Pacific Northwest Winter

Gift of the Stars

When Sera was young, she dreamed of touching the stars. It was all she ever wanted. As she grew up the dream became a yearning. So when she found herself at space academy after college, it wasn't a surprise to anyone that knew her. The big surprise was that she found Henri.

Henri hadn't planned to go into space. It was something that just happened to him. His younger brother wanted it. Phillip had dreamed of space, but space academy had not been a success for Phillip. The exercises made him sick and he had given up that dream.

But Henri... well, it wasn't his dream, but he found he enjoyed space academy. Even more than that, he had found love. No, not just love, but LOVE with a capital "L", in the form of one Sera Bakshi.

Sera and Henri married. They were on their honeymoon in Hawaii when they got the news. They were going to fulfill Sera's greatest dream; they were going to the space station. Everything went smoothly and here they were, facing their first Christmas together... in space.

Henri wanted to make it special for Sera. He loved everything about Christmas, from "O Tannenbaum" to "Silent Night". He had wonderful memories of Christmas and wanted to make new ones with Sera.

After handing the toothpaste to Sera, he brushed his teeth. He looked at her as she was doing the same, her hair fanned out from her head, almost like an old painting he had seen at the art museum. He smiled and winked at her.

Sera grinned and it expelled a small globule of toothpaste, which floated around until she managed to catch it on the end of her brush. She gave him a playful slap on the arm and he spun and floated away from her.

"How do you like being in space, Mrs. Sera Weber?" he asked her for the hundredth time. He was thrilled to share in her dream being fulfilled and he liked hearing the sound of her name mixing with his, that asking this always made him happy. He had tried to convince her to keep her maiden name. There had been several long discussions about: name changes, his and hers; no name changes; and name combinations, hers and his. In the end, she had insisted on being traditional and had taken his name. He would have been fine with any of it, but it still made him happy to hear it out loud.

"Space is no walk in the park, but I love it, Mr. Henri Weber," she replied for the hundredth time. She packed up her toothbrush and Velcroed the toothpaste back on the wall where they shared it.

Space was definitely no walk in the park. There were things that were just better with gravity: walking in the park, exercising, going to the bathroom, cooking, eating, well, just about every-

120

thing. When Sera looked out the window at the vastness of space and saw the Earth from this perspective, it was worth it. This was the most amazing thing and she would always cherish her experience on the space station.

She gave him a quick kiss and used his shoulders to propel herself through the door of the module. "Race you to the lab."

"Cheater," Henri said, as he tried to grab her leg, but continued floating away from her.

They worked on experiments throughout the day: tending the lettuce grown in Veggie, the plant growth unit; drawing blood, Henri was a little squeamish; growing bacteria; and hatching and studying fruit flies; just to name a few of the large array of experiments that were currently running.

While they worked Henri tried to come up with something special he could give to Sera. He had a small gift, but he had brought the same ginger bread tins for all the crew. He wouldn't be able to run to the store or order something online and they weren't able to bring a lot with them. He rummaged through his bonus food container to see if he could find something. He was down to his last two irradiated bratwurst. It wasn't Sera's favorite, so that wouldn't be a good gift for her. Besides, it was his favorite.

"Hey, Henri," Andre said. The Russian cosmonaut peered over his shoulder. "Anything good in there?"

"Bratwurst, dehydrated bananas, tuna fish, gnocchi and some hot cocoa."

"You have bratwurst?" Andre asked. "I'll trade. You like borscht?"

"With beef?" Henri asked.

"You bet." And before Henri could say another word, Andre had floated to his module to retrieve the borscht.

He didn't really want to trade his bratwurst, but he did like borscht and he had that second bratwurst. He was still debating the trade when Andre returned. The excited look on his face was enough to convince him to make the trade.

121

"You have more?"

"Last one." Henri tapped the package before closing his personal bonus container and replacing it on the rack. It would have been good with sauerkraut, but he had shared that one night and he had none left to eat with his last brat.

Just thinking about it made his mouth water. "Enjoy," he said as Andre headed off to his part of the Space Station.

He made his way to the exercise module of the space station where Sera was just finishing up on the treadmill. She reached for her towel and sopped up all the sweat clinging to her skin.

"You're glowing."

"I'm sweaty," she said. "Your turn, lazy bones."

"I'm not lazy; I've been busy."

"Doing what? Watching the sun rise and set half a dozen times?"

"A little," he admitted. "It's pretty cool. But I've been making friends with the Russians. We're doing a little negotiating."

"Oh yeah? What kind of negotiating."

"Trade negotiations," he said.

"What do you have to trade?" Sera wanted to know.

"Brats for borsht," he said.

"Those must have been some serious negotiations," Sera said. "I hope your sharing some with your wife."

"Maybe, if she's good," he said, giving her a wink and strapping into the treadmill.

For dinner Henri had the borsht.

"This is pretty good," he said. It was more gelatinous than what he was used to back on Earth. He scooped a spoonful and held it out to Sera. "Bite?"

Her mouth was full of fluffernutter tortilla wrap. She held up one finger and nodded as she swallowed. After taking the proffered spoon, she tried it. "That is good. Although, I'm still partial to my fluffernutter wraps. Too bad that was the last of my peanut butter."

"Maybe we could use the last of your marshmallow fluff on my last bratwurst," he said.

"Ugh, no!" Sera shook her head. "I don't even want to think about what that would taste like."

After the work day, they returned to their sleep stations and zipped up in their sleeping bags. Henri and Sera's stations were adjacent with Drew and Milo's sleep stations on either side. Andre and Yuri were in the Russian module. They had their heads oriented toward each other.

"Goodnight, Sera," Henri said.

"Goodnight, Henri," Sera said.

"Goodnight, John Boy," Drew said in a sing-song voice, before closing his station's door on their laughter.

The next day was Christmas Eve and there was an excited buzz on the station even by the Russian cosmonauts who would normally celebrate their Christmas in January. Of course, that meant there would be two celebrations, so that was another thing to look forward to. They would have the day off tomorrow, so it meant today would be extra busy checking systems and running any experiments that needed tending to.

"Tonight I'm having the seafood," Milo said. "It's traditional in Italy; for me, stuffed calamari, then linguini with clam sauce." He touched his pinched fingers to his lips and then opened his fingers up like a flower to show just how good it was going to be.

"Just cheese tortilla for me," Sera said. "I'm saving up for the turkey, yams and fresh baked crumb-free bread tomorrow and finish it off with a cup of hot cocoa."

"What, no fluffernutter?" Drew asked. He also shared Sera's penchant for the marshmallowy treat.

"All out of peanut butter," she sighed.

"Don't you have any fish?" Milo threw up his hands at the question and then took a sip of coffee from his mico gravity coffee cup. "Fish and then Mass. I have to do it or Nonna would be upset."

"I'll join you," Henri said. "I'll have a tuna fish tortilla wrap. Normally, we do pot roast on Christmas Eve, turkey or goose on Christmas day and gingerbread, maybe with some applesauce."

"Stop, you're making me hungry," Drew said, clutching his stomach.

"I have to go check on something." Sera pushed herself through the module's hatch and flew away.

Henri looked at her a little worried. He hadn't asked her much about her Christmas traditions. Did she even celebrate Christmas? He hoped he hadn't upset her somehow. He needed to do something special for her, but what?

Christmas music was playing in the background and Drew began whistling along with Dino to "A Marshmallow World". Henri smiled at the old fashioned song.

"Hey, Drew," he said. "You got any peanut butter left?"

"Yeah…, why?" Drew asked suspiciously.

"Any chance I could get it from you for Sera?"

"I don't know. Whadda ya got?"

"Um… tuna fish?" Henri suggested.

"Nah." Drew frowned, considering. "You got any of that brat-wurst left?"

Sera found Andre and Yuri at work in one of the Russian modules. They were speaking in Russian and, apparently, Yuri had said something funny, as Andre burst out laughing. They greeted her with a smile as she floated into the module.

"Good day to you," Andre said.

"Hey, Andre, Yuri," she began. "I was wondering if any of you had any special foods to trade?"

"No vodka." Yuri chuckled and shook his head.

"I got meat stew or fish," Andre said.

"I was actually thinking something more in the line of sauer-kraut?"

Christmas day, the crew was woken to the tune of "We Wish You a Merry Christmas". It wasn't a bad way to start the day. After morning ablutions, breakfast and some general hanging around, all the crew gathered to open their special Christmas box that had arrived a few days ago.

It contained apples and oranges for all, garlic, a tiny artificial tree, Santa hats and stockings with tiny candy canes, and a few other special items. They spent the day singing carols, making calls to family from space, and generally looking out the window at Earth.

Henri felt a pang of sadness after talking to Philip. He wished his brother could experience what he was seeing now. He had taken a lot of pictures to send home. It was the best he could do for Phillip. However, he wouldn't exchange being here with Sera for anything.

She floated up next to him looking like an elf and joined him at the window.

"It's amazing, isn't it?" Sera said.

"Yes, Sera," Henri agreed. "It truly is."

"Hard to believe we're really here for our first Christmas," she said.

"Do you do Christmas?" It seemed a stupid question to ask, since she had pinned a Santa hat to her head, but he needed to know.

She pointed to the hat. "Um, yeah."

"Well, I mean, when you're not in space," Henri said.

"Yes, Henri. I *do* Christmas."

He smiled at that. "Then, Merry Christmas, Sera." Henri pulled his Santa hat off and held it out.

Sera brought her hand from behind her back and handed Henri one of the Christmas stockings. "I re-used it," she explained.

She took the hat and pulled out a half-empty jar of peanut butter. She gave Henri a peculiar look.

"What's the matter? Don't you like it?" Henri asked. "I'm sorry. I shouldn't have given you something used, but I couldn't find a full one. I know how much you like your fluffernutters."

"It's not that." She nodded to the stocking in his hand.

He reached in and pulled out a can of food. He looked at her quizzically as he turned the can around to read the label: sauerkraut. Now it was Henri's turn to look dismayed. "Ah."

"I traded my marshmallow fluff for the sauerkraut," she said.

"And I traded my bratwurst, so you could have fluffernutters."

They looked at each other and grinned sheepishly as the peanut butter jar and sauerkraut can floated in the air next to them.

"Merry Christmas, Sera."

"Merry Christmas, Henri."

This would truly be a Christmas they would remember. They kissed in front of the big window looking out over earth with a background full of stars.

A Pacific Northwest Winter

Rain falling turns to snow
Bringing fantasies of a White Christmas
Midnight flurries turn to slush
Streets filled with white and grey Slurpees, lined with tire marks
Slushy streets turn to ice
Cars glide on streets like first time ice skaters
Business signs turn to 'Closed'
A lone street sander works over-time on melting ice
Icy streets turn to run off
Shoes walking outside, house cold, wet, wrinkled feet
Night snow turns lawns white
Children make snowmen with bits of grass and leaves and dirt
Snowmen turn to snow elves
Green lawns are sprinkled with the ruins of snow forts and
snow people
Cool temperatures turn up
It's another Green Christmas in the Pacific Northwest

Happy Holidays
from all of us
at the
Writers Cooperative
of the
Pacific Northwest!